Welcome to the Secret World of Alex Mack!

My friends and I were really excited about the pool party at Janie Robertson's house—until things went horribly wrong. A brush fire in the area is heading our way, and we're stranded alone at the house without any way to call for help! I *have* to use my powers to help us out of this emergency . . . but will I be able to keep the secret from my friends? Let me explain. . . .

I'm Alex Mack. I was just another average kid until my first day of junior high.

One minute I'm walking home from school—the next there's a *crash!* A truck from the Paradise Valley Chemical plant overturns in front of me, and I'm drenched in some weird chemical.

And since then—well, nothing's been the same. I can move objects with my mind, shoot electrical charges through my fingertips, and morph into a liquid shape . . . which is handy when I get in a tight spot!

My best friend, Ray, thinks it's cool—and my sister, Annie, thinks I'm a science project.

They're the only two people who know about my new powers. I can't let anyone else find out—not even my parents—because I know the chemical plant wants to find me and turn me into some experiment.

But you know something? I guess I'm not so average anymore!

The Secret World of Alex Mack™

Available from MINSTREL Books

NICKELODEON®

the secret world of

ALEX MACK ™

Pool Party Panic!

V.E. Mitchell

A MINSTREL® BOOK

Published by POCKET BOOKS
New York   London   Toronto   Sydney   Tokyo   Singapore

This book is a work of fiction. Names, characters, places and incidents are products of the author's imagination or are used fictitiously. Any resemblance to actual events or locales or persons, living or dead, is entirely coincidental.

A MINSTREL PAPERBACK *Original*

 A Minstrel Book published by
POCKET BOOKS, a division of Simon & Schuster Inc.
1230 Avenue of the Americas, New York, NY 10020

ISBN: 0-671-01428-5

First Minstrel Books printing June 1998

10 9 8 7 6 5 4 3 2 1

Cover art by Pat Hill Studio and Danny Feld

Printed in the U.S.A.

In memory of a very special four-footed friend

Mica
1988–1997

Whose main goal in life was
"supervising" her human,
but who didn't quite get this book finished.

Pool Party Panic!

CHAPTER 1

"Are you sure this is the right place?" Mrs. Mack eyed the entrance to Pedregoso Canyon nervously as she braked for the turn from the highway onto the narrow county road. She was taking Alex, Alex's friends Nicole Wilson and Robyn Russo, and her sister, Annie, to a pool party at Janie and Jeanette Robertson's house. Janie and Alex had become friends during their barely successful attempt to pass eighth-grade math. Jeanette, one of Annie's friends, was in college like Annie. She was very smart but a little short on common sense.

"I didn't realize the road was this bad," Mrs. Mack said.

Pedregoso Canyon—"Stony" Canyon—was narrow and boxlike. The mouth was barely wide enough for a two-lane county road beside the rocky creekbed. Large cottonwood trees and scrub willows grew along the watercourse. The tree limbs stretched across the road, almost brushing the roof of the car. "Yes, Mom," Alex said. "I'm sure this is the right place."

"I don't know . . ." Mrs. Mack gave the canyon an uncertain look. The road twisted and turned like a snake caught between the cliffs. "I didn't remember Janie's house being this far from town. Or there being only one road in or out of the canyon."

Nicole and Robyn, seated in the backseat with Alex, gave her questioning looks. Alex heaved an impatient sigh. "Mom! You say that every time you drive us out here."

Mrs. Mack frowned as she eased the car through a pair of tight S-curves. "That's because I forget this road really *is* as bad as I remember it. Are you sure you girls will be all right out here by yourselves?"

"Of course we will, Mom." Alex ran a hand through her dark blond hair. "The Robertsons have a *huge* pool. It's way too hot to do anything but hang out in the shallow end."

2

"With this heat, I really don't want to spend the weekend at home," Nicole added. "Our air conditioner broke Wednesday, and the repairman can't get to it until Monday."

"That's so totally typical." Robyn shuddered. "Our society is completely dependent on the reliable operation of technology, but everything fails when we need it most."

The car broke out of the trees as the canyon widened. Mrs. Mack squinted against the blazing sun, then slammed on the brakes. Two girls on matching bay horses ambled along the side of the road. For the next mile, rambling houses with broad lawns and well-kept grounds advertised the wealth of their owners.

"See. You're right, Mom," Annie said. "The Robertsons' house isn't that far from civilization."

"Uh—" Mrs. Mack swerved to avoid another horse and rider. The pavement took a sharp bend and cut back into the trees. "Why did Janie decide to have a party this weekend?"

"Because she just finished her lifeguard training," Alex said. "She invited a bunch of people to help her celebrate, but most of them were already busy."

Annie nodded. "Jeanette says they had to get their lifeguard certificates before they could have friends over to swim when their parents weren't home."

The canyon walls narrowed again, leaving barely enough room for the road and the creekbed. For the next five miles, the four girls kept up their chatter, discussing the heat wave and how nice it would be to spend the weekend in the Robertsons' pool. They didn't give Mrs. Mack time to notice the large space between the Robertsons' house and their nearest neighbor's.

The house was in a wide bowl at the end of the canyon. It was a two-story Mission-style building with a three-story tower on one end. An oval patch of lawn spread out from the main entrance. Black walnut trees planted by the original owner shaded most of the building. It was the oldest house in Pedregoso Canyon.

Mrs. Mack stopped the car at the front door. The girls spilled out of the car, grabbing their luggage and sleeping bags. As they sorted themselves out, Janie Robertson opened the front door. She was a rangy, coltish girl, her body made of planes and angles. Her frizzy brown hair was tied back with a faded scarf.

"Alex! Annie! You made it!" She flashed a wide, toothy smile at her guests as she circled to the driver's side of the car. "Mrs. Mack, thank you for letting Alex and Annie come. Passing my lifeguard test was really important to me."

"Alex hasn't talked about anything else since you called." Mrs. Mack beamed in response to Janie. "Do you think she might follow your example and work on her swimming?"

Alex felt her face start to glow. She leaned in the open window and gave her mom a quick peck on the cheek. "Bye, Mom. Thanks for the ride." She ducked her head out and hurried toward the house with her duffel bag. Annie waved at her mother, then grabbed the sleeping bags and followed her sister.

Janie's smile flickered briefly. "I don't know, Mrs. Mack. But if Alex wants any help, I'll be glad to give it to her."

"You do that. And please call us if you need anything this weekend. We can be here in under a half hour if necessary." Mrs. Mack started the car and backed down the driveway.

"Whew!" Nicole fanned her face. "Why the sudden parental concern, Alex? I thought she was going to make a last-minute offer to *stay* with us."

"Yeah." Alex, her face color back to normal, watched the car disappear. "She's been that way since we asked to come."

Annie shook her head. "Mom's really over-reacting. It's the first time she's let Alex do something like this, and she's nervous that something will go wrong."

Alex made a face at Annie, but Robyn nodded. "I totally understand. But it was already over a hundred when you guys picked me up, so who would have the energy to do anything?"

"At least it's cooler out here." Nicole glanced around. "I'd like to look around before it gets too hot."

"Sure," Janie said. "Why don't you take your stuff inside? We can do the tour as soon as the others get here."

While Robyn and Nicole were taking their bags inside, Janie's cousin Laura arrived. Alex knew Laura slightly. They had been in several classes together the past spring, but they had not talked much. Laura was a shorter version of her cousin, with the same frizzy brown hair and prominent front teeth.

Laura brought two friends with her. Tanya Wong was stocky and not very tall, with short, glossy black hair. Tanya had been Laura's best friend since grade school. Irina Kedrova was Laura's next-door neighbor. She was even shorter than Tanya, and her upper body was all muscle.

Her long, light brown hair faded to blond at the ends. She and her family had recently moved to the United States from a country that used to be part of Yugoslavia.

Once everybody was introduced and the bags put inside, Janie started the promised tour. "This area was part of one of the original Spanish land grants," she said. "The house was built much later, by a son or grandson of the first owner."

The house had thick walls of white-painted brick. Grilles of iron scrollwork covered all the windows. The original red tile roof was still in place on the tower, but on the two-story section, it had been replaced by redwood shingles. A small garage had been added to the tower end of the house, while a shed and a large garage with an attached carport stood beyond the pool.

"I liked the old tiles," Janie said, "but the roofer who replaced them said the structure couldn't support the weight anymore."

"That is strange." Irina's face wore a puzzled frown. Her words moved to a strange rhythm. "Many places in Europe have had this style of roof for many centuries."

Laura laughed. "The problem is, Uncle Ben hired somebody who didn't want to mess with the tile. So he made up a story about how the beams would break if he put new tiles up there."

Robyn shook her head. "Typical."

The group turned the corner and headed for the backyard. Although the day was hot, the shade from the walnut trees gave the illusion of coolness.

"Most of the old houses were well built, but some weren't." Tanya studied the house with a critical eye. "My mom's company remodels old houses. She says, for about thirty years, some buildings were made with wood that wasn't properly cured."

"You mean, the guy might have told the truth?" Janie asked.

Tanya shrugged. "It's hard to say. Most of those houses fell down ages ago, but some were repaired. Sort of. It depends on when the beams were replaced and how good the repair jobs were."

Robyn eyed the house nervously. "You mean, there's a chance the roof will fall in on us this weekend?"

"We could have an earthquake, too." Annie surveyed the trees and the canyon walls. "Or a flash flood. Or the house could burn down, or—"

"Annie! Must you?" Alex knew her sister was teasing Robyn, but sometimes Annie went a little too far.

"I could go on, if you like." Annie's expression was innocence itself. "The list of highly improbable disasters that *might* occur this weekend is quite long."

Alex rolled her eyes. "Annie, don't you and Jeanette have some *studying* to do?"

"Sure. As soon as I'm sure you won't get into any trouble." Annie smirked, waiting for the inevitable response to her teasing.

The younger girls groaned. "You said she *promised*." Nicole glared at Alex. "Is she going to hover over us all weekend?"

"Probably." *I'll never be able to face my friends again*, Alex thought. "She thinks she promised Mom to watch us every second."

They rounded the corner of the house and Irina gasped. The backyard was filled with a redbrick-and-cement patio surrounding a swimming pool. The pool was as long as a standard Olympic pool but at least twice as wide. At the far corner, a gazebo with latticed walls provided shade for several webbed chairs and lounges.

The water looked cool and inviting. Nicole knelt by the edge of the pool and let her hand trail in the water. "Don't worry about us, Annie," she said with a sigh. "We're not going anywhere."

Robyn located the sun relative to the house. A delighted smile broke across her face. "The pool is on the east side of the house. It'll be in shade most of the afternoon."

Janie grinned. "My granddad built it that way. On days like this, it's really great to go swimming without worrying about the afternoon sun."

Moving like a sleepwalker, Irina walked to the edge of the pool. She touched the water as if to assure herself it was real. "You have a pool like this, all for yourself? Back home, this would be for the entire team."

Laura touched Irina's shoulder. "*This* is home now. You can use the pool as much, or as little, as you like."

"Let me show you around inside." Janie started for the sliding door. "You can dump your stuff in the family room upstairs. Then we can go for a quick dip before lunch."

"Great!" Laura started for the door. "I was hoping you'd say that."

The door opened into a kitchen as big as Alex's living room. The stove was on an island in the middle of the room. A table and half a dozen chairs stood against the far wall. Beyond the kitchen was an elegant dining room and a living room that belonged on the cover of a magazine. "This is my mother's part of the house," Janie said. "Heaven help us if we mess it up."

After the girls collected their bags, Janie led them upstairs. The family room was as informal as the downstairs was formal. It had large windows looking out over the swimming pool and the hills behind the house. Alex hadn't realized how low the canyon walls were here. She wandered to the window for a better look.

"That's some view, isn't it?" Tanya joined Alex at the window. "On a clear day, you can see the higher peaks. I'll bet it's a lot cooler up there today."

"Higher peaks? I don't see anything but haze." Alex searched the horizon, trying to figure out what Tanya was talking about. The baked hills quickly faded into a metallic brightness that made her eyes hurt. It was so hazy that she couldn't even see Surveyor's Ridge, which wasn't *that* far to the north.

"Usually, you see them after a rainstorm." Janie crossed to the window. "The view from Dad's office, up in the tower, is really great!"

"Hey, guys!" Jeanette entered the room. She was as tall as her younger sister, but she moved with more grace. Her hair was several shades darker than Janie's. She went over to Annie. "Did you want to go swimming first, or just get to work?"

Annie looked down on the sun-splashed pool. "I'd just as soon get to work. We've got a lot of stuff to go over, and I don't really want to get sunburned."

"My room is down the hall. Grab your books and let's get started." Annie collected her things and the two girls left.

"All right!" Nicole slapped Alex's palm. "That's the end of our baby-sitters."

"Not quite," Laura said. "Jeanette's room is on this side of the house. They can see everything that happens in the pool."

"That's all right," Alex said. "Once Annie gets her nose in a book, she doesn't notice anything until it falls on her."

"Yes!" Tanya raised her fist triumphantly. "What are we waiting for?"

CHAPTER 2

The water felt wonderful, Alex thought as she floated in the shade near the house. A few puffy clouds wafted overhead. Nicole drifted nearby, holding on to the side with one hand. Robyn had retreated indoors, afraid she would get sunburned even though she was thoroughly smeared with sunblock. Tanya was napping in the shade. Janie, Laura, and Irina were racing each other on the far side of the pool. Shouts of "Butterfly," "Backstroke," and "Freestyle" punctuated their laps. Janie and her cousin were evenly matched, but Irina usually finished at least a body's length ahead of the other two.

"Where do they get all that energy?" Nicole

made a lazy roll toward Alex. "It's way too hot to do anything."

The late afternoon was miserably hot, with the humidity rising faster than the temperature. "Beats me." Alex pulled herself around to get a better view of the racers. "It must have something to do with getting carried away by what you're doing."

"Not me. Not on a day like this." Nicole shook her head. "That much exercise isn't healthy when it's this hot."

"I totally agree." Ice cubes tinkled as Robyn set a tray by the edge of the pool. "I made some lemonade for anyone who's interested."

"Definitely!" Alex hauled herself out of the pool. Turning, she sat on the edge, her feet dangling in the water. Nicole pulled herself up beside Alex. Both helped themselves to tall glasses.

"Hey, everybody!" Robyn called. "I've got lemonade."

The racers tagged the far wall and pushed off toward Robyn. As usual, Irina was first. The three pulled themselves out of the water, and Tanya joined the group. "Thanks, Robyn," Janie said. "We were working harder out there than I thought."

The girls sipped their lemonade as the three

14

racers caught their breath. "You're really good, Irina," Alex said. "Where did you learn to swim like that?"

"I was on the swim team for my country for many years." She blinked and rubbed her eyes. "I trained for the Olympics until my family moved to this country."

"The Olympics? Wow!" Janie's eyes widened. "That's unreal. I *wish* I was that good."

"It is hard work. Many hours of practice are required." Irina looked around the patio, her gaze resting longest on the pool. "But you have a beautiful place. All to yourself, with no one to compete with you for it. You can practice all the time."

Alex copied Irina's appraisal. It *was* a beautiful pool. The redbrick pavement around it provided a dramatic contrast to the blue water. The greater-than-standard width gave the swimmers a lot of extra room to work out or to float. Colored tile on the walls and bottom created the illusion of looking into an undersea garden. Alex wondered if someone floating near the wall had ever been mistaken for part of the design.

Janie laughed. "If practice was all I needed, I might stand a chance."

Nicole nodded. "At our school, you'll learn,

you have to be buddies with the coach if you want to stay on the team. McAllister and I got into a big fight at tryouts. After that, I didn't have a prayer."

Tanya started giggling. "I remember that. Coach McAllister gave the wrong directions, but she wasn't about to listen to you correct her."

Laura stretched and squeezed the water from her hair. "That's right. She was so mad her face matched her red hair. I don't think she liked you laughing at her, either, Tanya."

"But it *was* funny. She looked like she was about to explode." Giggling even harder, Tanya climbed to her feet. With one hand planted on her hip, she swaggered over to her best friend. In a shrill voice, she scolded Laura. "You over there! Shake the water out of your ears and pay attention! I don't give you directions just to hear my own voice!"

Tanya's performance was so good that Alex could see the swimming coach. Mrs. McAllister was one of the least-liked teachers in the school district—and also one of the best known. In addition to coaching the girls' swim team, she taught swimming for most of the schools in Paradise Valley.

Nicole stretched out on the wet bricks, putting

her hands behind her head. "However you look at it, I don't belong on *her* team. I was lucky to find it out *before* I wasted a lot of time trying to fit in."

"So that's why you didn't qualify," Alex said. "I always wondered what happened."

"I wasn't actually good enough to make the team. But McAllister's attitude convinced me it wasn't worthwhile hanging around as an alternate. She would have been on my case every minute."

"She's that way with everybody," Laura said. "You get used to it after a while."

Nicole shrugged. "It's a lot easier to put up with that when there's a payoff. If I'm going to knock myself out for minimal return, it might as well be on math."

Alex finished her lemonade and lay down beside Nicole. The rough bricks pressed into her bare legs and shoulders. She noticed that overhead the puffy clouds were colliding to form dense gray masses. To the north, thicker black clouds boiled up near the mountains. A gust of wind kicked up a cloud of dust, danced through the leaves on the walnut trees, and brushed a chilly finger across Alex's damp skin.

She sat up to get a better look at the clouds.

"Janie?" Alex pointed toward the mountains. "It looks like we may have a thunderstorm later."

Janie looked to the north. "Oh, no! That will totally mess up the TV reception."

"What's so important about that?" Robyn glanced nervously at the clouds.

"Channel Thirty-Seven is having a tacky beach flicks marathon tonight," Janie answered. "I thought it would be fun to watch, considering how hot it's been."

"Do you mean tacky beach flicks as in nineteen fifties surfside romances?" Nicole rolled her eyes. "How retro!"

Janie shrugged. "It's that or the late-night creature feature. Take your pick."

Laura snorted. "Some choice. Isn't your dad ever going to get a satellite dish so you can get more channels out here?"

"Not a chance. If it were up to him, we wouldn't even have a television." Janie pushed herself to her feet. "I don't know about you guys, but I'm getting hungry. Shall we fix dinner?"

"Yeah." "Great idea." "Suits me." The girls' answers overlapped each other. They scrambled to their feet, and Robyn picked up the tray with the lemonade. As they headed inside, the mutter of distant thunder rolled down from the mountains.

Totally predictable, Alex thought. As soon as she and her friends had baked the pizza and thrown together a salad, Annie and Jeanette appeared. "I can't believe you forgot those notes, Annie," Jeanette said as they entered the kitchen. "They are absolutely *critical* for what we're doing."

"How was I to know you'd loaned yours out?" Annie glared at Jeanette with an annoyed expression that Alex knew too well.

Jeanette shrugged off Annie's comment and walked over to the stove. She examined the dinner with a critical eye. "Mom said you were supposed to serve the zucchini with the pizza. And you should have made twice that much salad."

"We voted." Janie looked her sister in the eye. "Nobody wanted zucchini. And if you don't like the salad, talk to Robyn and Alex. They made it."

Alex put on her best *do-you-really-want-to-discuss-this?* look. "We can always make more. I was just going by how hungry people said they were."

After a moment, Jeanette shrugged. "I don't care, as long as I don't have to explain it to Mom.

She made me promise to see that everyone followed her menu plans."

A wicked grin spread across Laura's face. "But, Jeanette," she said to her cousin, "don't you know that athletes need protein and carbohydrates after a heavy workout?"

Annie, standing next to Jeanette, struggled to hide a grin. "I think you're outmaneuvered, Jeanette. If you really want the zucchini, you can cook it. Otherwise, I'd say the majority wins."

The girls loaded their plates and trooped upstairs to the family room with the extra pizza and the salad bowl. Alex glanced through the windows before finding a place on the floor. The clouds had condensed into towering black masses with dazzling white tops. The wind blew in gusts, sending waves through the dried grass on the hills above the house. The walnut trees shook until their leaves were a blur of motion. Rows of thunderheads marched toward them. Far to the north, Alex thought she saw a flash of lightning.

Janie picked up the remote and began flipping channels. The picture from Channel 37 was lost in static and snow. The reception was equally poor for the two other channels that were showing movies. Only Paradise Valley Public TV was putting out a strong enough signal to punch through the interference of the approaching storm.

" 'Better Living Through Chemistry'?" Robyn asked when she saw what the program was. "*Puh-lease.* Like I'm supposed to believe everything the chemical plant says about itself."

"It looks like a good show," Annie said. "Leave it on while we eat."

Alex figured Robyn was right about the program being more an advertisement for the chemical plant than a real documentary. She scooted closer to Robyn and Nicole, leaving her sister and Jeanette to watch the television.

At first, conversation was minimal as the girls attacked the pizza. With four different types, Alex had to hustle to get a second piece of her favorite, Canadian bacon and pineapple. The salad, however, found no takers except Robyn and Jeanette.

"At Paradise Valley Chemical, we believe in progress at any cost." The background murmur of the television was broken by static. "We work night and day to eliminate all obstacles that keep us from reaching that goal. Our next segment will profile the dedicated researchers who have developed, in record time, a line of chemicals that will revolutionize firefighting forever."

Tanya shot a poisonous look at the screen. "This is getting really old. Don't you have any videos we can watch?"

Laura snorted. "Sure, if you like bad science-fiction. Uncle Ben is really big on nineteen fifties sci-fi movies."

"What do you have available?" Irina asked.

Jeanette groaned. "I've seen everything we have at least ten times. I really can't face watching *The Day the Earth Stood Still* again."

Robyn's forehead wrinkled in concentration. "Isn't that one of the few movies from that period that's any good?"

"Try watching it five times in a row," Janie said. "Dad wanted to make sure we appreciated the artistic style of the cinematography."

"You're kidding," Alex said. *Nobody* watched a movie that many times in a row. "Aren't you?"

Janie and Jeanette shook their heads until their frizzy curls bounced like the television picture. "No!" they said in unison.

Jeanette looked at Annie. "Why don't we go into town and rent something with decent special effects? We could also pick up some ice cream on the way home."

Annie frowned. "I don't think that's a good idea. We promised to be around in case we were needed. That doesn't include running into town."

"What could go wrong?" Jeanette asked. "It only takes an hour to grab some videos and get home. We could even pick up those notes you forgot. Who wants to see *Jurassic Park?*"

"Me!" "Me!" "Me!"

"What about getting *Batman*, too?"

"Or *Blade Runner?*"

"Or all the *Star Wars* movies? We could have an outer-space marathon."

"Please, Annie. Aren't your notes really important?" Alex shot her sister a pleading look. "Besides, what could go wrong in an hour?"

Nearby lightning sent a blizzard of snow across the television, and the sound broke up into static. Annie glanced toward the flickering screen, then back to her sister. Her shoulders sagged in defeat. "Alex, if Mom finds out about this, she'll ground both of us."

As if we have any intention of doing anything, Alex thought. To reassure her sister, she lifted her hand, palm outward. "I promise, Annie. We'll stay right here and watch—something— until you get back."

Solemn nods echoed Alex's promise. "I still think this is a bad idea," Annie muttered as she went to grab her windbreaker.

Annie's doubts increased when she and Jeanette left the house. The wind had picked up, tossing the tree branches into ominous motion. Dust and grit bit at her exposed skin. The bass grumble of the thunder sounded much louder and closer than it had indoors. "Are you sure we should be doing this, Jeanette?" She had to shout to be heard over the wind and thunder.

"Not to worry." Jeanette dashed under the carport and opened the passenger's door of a battered two-door sedan. She slid across the seat, fastened her seat belt, and put the key in the ignition. "Hurry up, Annie. Get in."

Annie swallowed nervously. The car looked as if it had seen better days. Still, she *had* agreed to go into town with Jeanette. They really did need the physics notes she had forgotten. Though at different schools, they both had similar summer research. Reluctantly, she climbed in. "Are you sure this thing will hold together long enough to get us there and back?"

"No problem." Jeanette turned the key as Annie struggled with the stubborn buckle on her seat belt. On the fourth try, the engine finally caught. Pulling the car out of the carport, Jeanette spun it in a tight circle that sprayed rocks from under the tires. She gunned the engine and raced toward the road. "All right! Let's see how fast we can do this!"

Annie braced herself against the dash and held on. *I have a very bad feeling about this*, she thought. She never should have agreed to go with Jeanette.

CHAPTER 3

"Well, guys," said Alex, "what do we want to watch until they get back?"

Janie pointed toward the oversize entertainment center. A double set of doors covered the shelves beneath the television. "Dad stores his videotapes there. I guess we can take a vote."

The girls looked at one another, checking to see who would make the decision. A gust of wind whipped loose twigs against the window. A low grumble of thunder rolled through the silence.

Laura shrugged. "I've seen all of Uncle Ben's collection too many times. Let someone else decide."

Irina opened the cabinet and started reading

the titles. "I know of these, but I have not seen them. Which is the best one?"

"That depends." Janie tugged at the ends of her hair. "Most of them are pretty tacky. But even the quality flicks get old if you watch them too much."

Laura nodded. "She's right. Uncle Ben wears his tapes out, he watches them so many times."

Alex knelt beside the cabinet. "Wow! Your dad must have every nineteen fifties sci-fi movie ever made." She shuffled through the tapes. "Unless someone has a strong preference, why don't we let Irina pick something?"

Irina touched a tape, then pulled her hand back. "I would not know which to choose. And I would prefer to pick something that everyone likes."

"Well, most of them are so bad they're kind of funny. Especially the ones with the phony special effects." Alex took out the tape Irina had reached for and was relieved to see what she had picked. *"Forbidden Planet* is pretty cool, especially for when it was made. Does anybody mind watching it?"

Robyn and Nicole shook their heads. Janie and Laura looked at each other. Laura shrugged. "I guess that's as good as any. At least I haven't seen it recently."

Alex took the tape from its case and plugged it into the VCR. She hit the Play button and stretched out on the floor.

Janie stood. "I'll go make some popcorn. You can't watch a movie without popcorn."

"I'll help." Laura scrambled to her feet and started for the stairs. She lowered the room lights on her way out. "The rest of you can keep on watching. We'll be right back."

"Are you sure?" Alex asked. "We can wait until you get back."

"We've got every movie in that cabinet memorized," Laura said. "We won't miss a thing."

"Don't worry about them," Tanya said in a low voice as the cousins escaped. "They really do know them all by heart."

Alex heard pots clanging in the kitchen, followed shortly by popping sounds. Before long, the heavenly aroma of freshly made popcorn floated up the stairs. Even though she had just finished dinner, the smell made Alex's mouth water.

Outside, the wind picked up, whistling around the eaves and rattling the windows. Alex glanced nervously toward the windows, suddenly realizing how dark it was outside. The heavy clouds blanketed the sky, turning the long summer evening to night.

A brilliant flash lit up the room. It was followed by a deafening crack. The television and the room lights went out. Irina screamed and curled into a tight ball, her arms wrapped around her head.

"What happened?" "Is everything all right?" "That was too close for comfort." The girls' words tangled together and overlapped.

"Stay put," Janie shouted from downstairs. "We're bringing flashlights."

Alex blinked to clear away the afterimages. When her eyes adjusted, there was enough light to make out her surroundings. Irina was still huddled in a tight ball. Alex crawled over to her and touched her shoulder. "Are you okay? It was only the lightning."

Slowly Irina unfolded from her defensive position. "It was so loud. So close. Like artillery shells . . ."

"Artillery shells? You mean, like in the movies?" Alex frowned. It seemed a long stretch to confuse the thunder with special sound effects Alex had heard in movie theaters.

Irina took several deep breaths. "More like . . .

evening news. Sometimes, where I lived *was* the evening news."

Robyn slid closer. "You mean, you were, like, in the middle of the fighting they show on television here? With people bombing whole cities?"

Irina's nod was highlighted by a more distant flash of lightning. "When my country declared independence from Yugoslavia, not everyone was happy. My parents sent me to live in a small town with my grandmother. Even in that place, there was fighting and civil war." She shuddered at the memory.

"Going on all around you?" Nicole asked. "How did you end up in Paradise Valley?"

"My mother is a chemist. She gave a talk at a big meeting last year. People from the chemical plant heard her and offered her a job."

"So you just left everything and moved here? To boring old Paradise Valley?" Robyn sounded like she was having trouble with the leap of faith required to make such a move. "Weren't you afraid to leave everything behind?"

"My family is here now. Everything else . . ." Irina's body was silhouetted by the glow of flashlights coming up the stairs. She lifted her shoulders in an exaggerated shrug. "If a bomb lands on one's apartment, there is nothing left anyway. It is better in this country."

Janie and Laura entered with the flashlights and two large bowls of popcorn. With enough light to see by, the girls arranged themselves in a circle around the popcorn. Janie switched off her flashlight, leaving Laura's to light the room.

Irina looked around the circle, her gaze remaining longer on Tanya and Nicole. "Here everyone can be friends, even when people are different. It is much better than fighting to make everyone alike."

Robyn shuddered. "What a depressing thought. I would hate it if everybody was just like me."

Nicole patted her on the shoulder. "We'd all hate it, if we were all exactly like you. That would be *really* boring."

"Like being you wouldn't be boring?" Robyn asked with an edge in her voice, even though she had been the one to bring up the well-worn argument.

"At least I'm boring in my own way." Nicole sounded so smug that Alex knew she was teasing Robyn to provide a change of subject.

Since moving the discussion away from Irina's past seemed like a good idea, Alex scrambled to find a new topic. "Did anybody do something interesting with their vacation this summer? Something besides staying around here?"

"Well, I spent a month in Florida visiting my grandmother," Tanya said.

"Florida?" Nicole said. "That sounds really cool."

"It was okay, but she lives in Jacksonville." Tanya shrugged. "One big city is like any other."

Alex frowned. A vacation in Florida ought to be really exciting. "Didn't you get to do anything fun?"

"On the weekends, mostly, when she didn't have to be on call. She's a doctor. We went down to Orlando several times, and I almost got through everything at Universal Studios. We also went to Sea World a couple of times."

"You spent an entire month in Florida touring theme parks?" Nicole demanded in disbelief. "Shouldn't you have done something besides wasting your money on frivolous entertainment?"

"Well, actually . . ." Tanya grinned sheepishly. "Both Gran and I really like the rides. But she also made sure I saw more than enough museums and stuff. We did that on the days when she was on call. Then if she needed to go to the clinic for an emergency, she was available."

"Tell us all about it," Alex said. "I've never

been to Florida, and my parents never get around to taking us to any of the amusement parks around here.''

The other girls seconded Alex's request. With everyone hanging on to her words, Tanya described her trips to Universal Studios, Sea World, and the Kennedy Space Center, as well as what she had seen in other parts of Florida. While she talked, the thunderstorm provided a backdrop of light and sound effects.

Despite Jeanette's promises not to waste time, she poked through every movie in the video store before finally renting *Jurassic Park*, *Blade Runner*, and *Batman*. By then, Annie was so mad she could barely talk. She kept watching the storm through the plate-glass window, afraid that they would have trouble getting up the narrow canyon if the wind blew down any trees. If only she hadn't forgotten those notes! Then Jeanette couldn't have talked her into this trip. Her only lucky break so far was that her parents had already left for the evening when Jeanette circled by the Mack house for Annie to grab the notes. Otherwise, they would have had to return after they went to the video store.

''Quit worrying,'' Jeanette said after Annie's

third request to hurry. "Nothing will happen. Those trees have been there forever."

"All the more reason to expect this wind to blow something down," Annie replied. "Besides, we said we'd be back as soon as possible. This is taking *way* too long."

"Don't be silly. I'm sure our sisters can look out for themselves and their friends."

"That isn't the point, Jeanette, and you know it! We said we would be back quickly. They might worry if we take too long."

With a sigh of frustration, Jeanette took the movies to the counter. After paying for them, she followed Annie from the store. "I don't see any problem. They knew how many stops we had to make. You don't really think they'll miss us, do you?"

"That's still not the point. We promised to be there in case we were needed." Realizing it would do her no good to continue the argument, Annie fastened her seat belt. While they were buying the ice cream, she limited her comments to telling Jeanette what flavors Alex and her friends preferred.

By the time they were out of town, the lightning was dancing around the mountains to the north and the wind was blowing hard. It was the worst storm Annie remembered in the last several summers. The wind blew dust into the car through the passenger window. Annie tried to close it, but the window wouldn't roll all the way up. Before long, she was sneezing.

A couple of miles out of town, a funny noise started. It sounded like they were driving over a washboard. At the same time, the car swerved toward the center of the road. "Pull over!" Annie shouted. "Stop the car!"

"Don't panic! I've got it under control," Jeanette answered, fighting the wheel.

"Pull over," Annie said in a calmer tone. "I think you've got a flat."

"How would you know?" The car jerked and shimmied as Jeanette tried to straighten the wheel. "You're not driving."

"Our car acted the same way when Dad had a flat a couple of months ago."

"Yeah, sure." Nevertheless, Jeanette slowed the car and pulled it off the road. The car coasted to a stop. "If you're so sure it's a flat, why don't you check it out, Annie?"

"Right." Annie wrestled the door open. Between the wind and the stubborn hinge, it was a close contest. The door rebounded, hitting Annie on the legs when she turned to ask Jeanette for a flashlight. "Ouch!"

"Hurry up and close the door," Jeanette said as she handed Annie the flashlight. "You're letting in too much dust."

"Thanks for the vote of confidence." Annie slammed the door. She thumbed the switch on the flashlight, but nothing happened. By touch, she unscrewed the top and shook the case. It was empty. "Great. No batteries."

Jeanette had left the car running. Annie glanced to the front and rear. The headlights scattered enough light that she could tell the flat wasn't on this side. Cautiously, she moved behind the car and peeked along the driver's side. The rear tire was all right, but the front one, as Annie had suspected, was sitting on its rim.

Retracing her path, Annie opened the passenger door. She tossed the flashlight on the seat. "Do you have one that works? The front tire on your side is flat."

"What good is a flashlight?" Jeanette asked. "There's nothing we can do anyway."

CHAPTER 4

Annie stared at Jeanette in disbelief. "We need the flashlight to see with, so we can change the tire."

"What do you mean?" Jeanette looked at Annie like she was crazy. "We'll have to wait for someone to help us."

"No way!" Annie gave the deserted road a pointed look. "How many people do you expect to stop on a night like this?"

"It only takes one. Sooner or later, someone always stops."

"You mean, this isn't the first time this has happened?" Annie rolled her eyes. "Then why don't you have a working flashlight? If you've had flat tires before, you should be equipped to change them."

Jeanette stared at her blankly. "I don't know how to change a flat. I always get someone to help me."

"Oh, great!" Annie pawed through her pack for her flashlight. It was a little one that ran on only one battery, but she had replaced it recently. She hoped it would give her enough light to do the job. "I don't feel like waiting to be rescued. So turn off the car and come help me."

"Why can't we just wait?" Jeanette glanced nervously at the storm off to the north. "I'm sure it won't be long."

Annie reached over and turned off the ignition. "I hope you're right, but I don't want to test your theory. Let's get started, and we'll be that much farther along if someone stops."

Reluctantly, Jeanette climbed out of the car. She opened the trunk, then watched while Annie pulled out the spare and the jack. Jeanette eyed the jack with distaste. "You don't really expect me to use that, do you?"

"Do you expect the car to lift itself up?" Annie carried the tools to the front of the car. Leaving them there, she searched beside the road until she found some big rocks to block the rear wheels. With Jeanette still watching her as if she were crazy, Annie blocked the wheels and started jacking up the car.

By the time Annie had enough clearance to work on the lug nuts, she noted the road was still deserted. The nuts were so tight she began wishing someone *would* come along to help. However, she was more determined than ever not to wait for a rescue that might not come. She leaned all her weight against the tire iron to break the nuts free. Jeanette helped with the last one.

Annie lifted the spare from the trunk and rolled it to the front of the car. When she got a good look at it, she knew they were in trouble. The spare was low on air, too low to take them more than a few miles. In fact, considering Jeanette's driving, they would be lucky to make it back to town. "When was the last time you checked your spare?"

"I don't know. It was good the last time I used it."

"That figures. It's going flat, too." Annie rolled her eyes again. Jeanette's approach to car maintenance seemed extremely casual. Annie doubted that Jeanette would have noticed any problem with the spare before it went completely flat, too. Since the traffic that evening was so light, they would have to put it on and try to make it to the Macks' house. She didn't want to think what her parents would say when they got home.

"If it's flat, too, what will we do?" Jeanette asked.

Annie leaned against the jack handle. It was hard work raising the car the last few inches. She pulled the tire off and rolled it to the side. After putting the spare in place, she started replacing the lug nuts. "We'll have to go to my house. My parents went out for the evening, but my dad can help us when they get home."

"But what about the tire?" Jeanette asked. "I can't drive on a flat."

"The spare should be all right, if you go slow." Annie threw her weight against the tire iron to tighten a nut. "Besides, I'm not sure you should trust my work here."

"Why's that?"

"I may not be getting these nuts tight enough." She switched to another nut. "But there hasn't been any traffic in the last half hour, which is really weird. We have to get closer to town. Then, even if your spare goes completely flat, we can walk somewhere to get help."

"Walk?" Jeanette shook her head. "I'll stay with the car. *You* can walk, if you want to."

"Whatever." Annie decided to concentrate on changing the tire. It didn't seem like she and Jeanette were going to agree on anything concerning the best way to get out of this mess.

The girls were so interested in hearing about Tanya's vacation that they lost track of the time. It wasn't until Tanya reached the end of her story that Alex thought to look at her watch. It was after eleven o'clock. "Why aren't Annie and Jeanette back by now?" she asked. "Could something have gone wrong?"

Janie frowned as she realized how long the older girls had been gone. "We can look for their headlights from my dad's study."

Laura gave a knowing laugh. "Jeanette probably had another flat tire. You know how she takes care of her car."

"Not!" Tanya giggled. "She'd better find a boyfriend who can keep that junker running, since she couldn't recognize the business end of a screwdriver to save her own life."

"Not funny." Alex glared at the circle of faces. "Having car trouble in a storm like this isn't something to laugh about."

"Do you mean Jeanette is permitted to drive

a vehicle that she cannot repair?'' Irina asked, frowning.

Laura shrugged. "If it's math or physics, Jeanette is absolutely *brilliant*. But if it's something practical, she needs a baby-sitter worse than any three-year-old.''

Janie picked up her flashlight. "Why don't we go look for the car, Alex? The rest of you can stay here. That way, we won't all be tromping around Dad's office.''

At the end of the hall, a circular staircase led upward. Mr. Robertson's office occupied the top floor of the tower. It had large windows facing every direction. Toward the road, all Alex could see was the dark sea of trees, tossed by the wind and highlighted by flashes of lightning. There was no trace of anything that might be headlights.

Alex walked over to the northeast window. The storm still raged in the mountains, and it was moving toward them. Although a strong wind was blowing, it hadn't started to rain yet.

Janie joined Alex. "I don't like this storm. It's been so hot and dry, the lightning could start a brush fire.''

"Are we in any danger?'' The storm didn't seem that close, but Janie's suggestion was scary.

Alex had seen several TV shows about forest fires, and they seemed extremely dangerous.

"I doubt it. Nothing has reached this house since it was built in the late seventeen hundreds." The glow from the flashlight gave Janie's face a sinister look. "But my dad always worries about things that *might* happen. I guess the habit is contagious."

The telephone rang. Both girls jumped, and Janie almost dropped the flashlight. Catching herself, she picked up the phone. After listening a minute, she handed it to Alex. "It's Annie."

"What happened?" Alex asked. "We expected you back a while ago."

"That's a long story," Annie answered. "Jeanette had a flat tire, and her spare was low, too. We barely made it home."

"What did Mom and Dad say?" After all the work it had taken to get permission to stay at Janie's, Alex figured her parents would be furious at the older girls for leaving.

"Well . . . they're not home yet." Annie's tone told Alex that her sister shared her fears. "I guess Dad will have to help us get the tire fixed when he gets here. I was afraid the car wouldn't make it across town to Drago's truck stop. T

43

the only place that might have a repairman working at this hour."

"Are you sure?"

"No." There was a long pause. "But that's our best shot tonight. The other choice is to have Dad drive us back out, but he'd probably insist on bringing everybody home."

"Or stay out here, in case we needed the car." To Alex, having her father at the Robertsons' house didn't sound like much fun.

"Whatever." Annie paused. "Is everything all right out there? Janie sounded a bit rattled when she answered the phone."

"It startled us. That's all. The power went out, so the house is really quiet. Except for the storm." A flash of lightning, much closer than the others, lit up the wind-tossed trees. The bass rumble of thunder boomed in its wake.

"Wow! I heard that," Annie said. "Are you sure you guys are all right out there? With the storm and no power?"

"We're fine, Annie." Alex nibbled on her lower lip. "Although Janie said the lightning might start a brush fire. Do you think that's likely?"

"Well . . ." There was a long pause while Annie considered the situation. "I suppose it *could* happen, but I wouldn't worry about it. Besides, the sheriff's department will evacuate everyone before there's any danger. Or you guys could all hide in the swimming pool. With that much water and the brick patio around it, it's got to be the safest place in that canyon."

"Thanks, Annie." Alex heaved a sigh of relief. Annie's words put the situation into proper perspective. Janie had said no fire had ever reached here. Still, being reminded that the authorities had plans for even the most unlikely emergencies was comforting. It meant she really didn't have to worry about it. "I'm sure you're right. Hurry up and get back with the ice cream."

"You bet. And while we're waiting for Dad, I'll keep an eye on the news to make sure the storm doesn't cause any more damage than it already has."

"Okay, Annie. We'll see you in a bit. Bye."

"Bye, Alex."

Reluctantly Alex hung up the phone. She would never admit it to Annie, but not having the older girls around made her a little nervous. It would be different when she got her driver's license. Then she wouldn't have to worry about being stuck somewhere without transportation. Of course, even a license wouldn't have helped now. Jeanette and Annie had taken the only vehicle. Whatever happened, they were stuck out at the end of a canyon.

Alex shook her head, angry at herself. The power outage and the storm were getting to her. She was imagining disasters to fill the unfamiliar circumstances.

"When will they be back?" Janie asked as they started down the stairs. The flashlight bobbed with each step, making irregular, jerky patterns of light and darkness on the walls.

"Annie wasn't sure. She said Jeanette's spare has a leak, too." Alex reached for the handrail to keep her balance in the confusion of twisting shadows. "They're waiting for my dad to get home so he can take them to Drago's to get it fixed. If possible."

Janie shook her head. "They only have one guy there after ten on Saturday nights. Jeanette has done this before."

"Oh, great. I'll bet my dad will insist on taking us all back to my house. My parents only let me come because Annie and Jeanette were going to be here to watch out for us." Alex followed Janie through the door to the second-floor hall.

"Jeanette?" Janie laughed. "My sister has ab-

solutely *no* practical skills. She needs more looking after than any of us."

"You mean, she does stuff like this with the
flat tires all the time?" Alex frowned, wondering
how Jeanette managed to get away with such
carelessness. Her parents expected her and
Annie to learn from their mistakes and not re-
peat them.

"Pretty bad, isn't it?"

They entered the family room. The other girls
began questioning them immediately.

"Did you see them?"

"I'll bet Jeanette had another flat tire."

"Who was on the phone?"

"When will they get back with the ice cream?"

Janie held up her hand for silence. "Laura's
right. Jeanette had a flat, and Annie insisted they
go back to her house. Until they get the tire
fixed, they aren't going anywhere."

"Unless my dad decides we shouldn't be out
here alone." Alex's words were greeted by a
chorus of groans. "After all, Annie and Jeanette
promised to be here in case of emergency."

Nicole nodded. "Alex is right. We did agree
to having them in charge this weekend. So we
probably shouldn't have let them go into town,

even if we did want to see some different movies."

"Well, there's nothing we can do about it now." Tanya yawned. "After that workout this afternoon, I'm tired. I vote we get our sleeping bags and sack out. At least until Alex's father insists on spoiling our party."

Laura and Irina seconded Tanya's proposal. Alex didn't feel particularly sleepy, but she wasn't sure how long the batteries in the flashlights would last. Getting her sleeping bag laid out now seemed like a good thing to do. She and her friends could talk just as well after they were ready for bed. In fact, half the fun of a slumber party was to get into bed and then talk half the night.

Alex was more tired than she thought. Once she was in her sleeping bag and the flashlights were turned off, she began to feel drowsy. She and Laura discussed the English class they were going to be taking, and Robyn observed they had been assigned to the worst teacher in the school. Before long, the breaks in the conversation lengthened, and the girls drifted to sleep.

The sound of coughing awakened Alex. It took

her a few moments to realize it was Robyn. "What's wrong?" she whispered.

"The smoke," Robyn answered between coughs. "It's bothering my allergies."

Smoke? Alex took a deep breath, feeling the sharp bite in her nose and throat. She must have been breathing the smoke for quite a while before Robyn woke her up. "I smell it, too. I wonder why the smoke alarm didn't go off."

"I don't know. Maybe the Robertsons don't have one."

"Maybe." That didn't seem likely, though. Alex crawled over to Janie and shook her shoulder. "Janie, wake up! Something's on fire!"

CHAPTER 5

Janie groaned and rubbed her eyes. "What is it, Alex?" she mumbled sleepily.

Robyn coughed harder. That coughing spell was longer than the one that woke Alex. *How bad is Robyn's allergy to smoke?* Alex wondered. She wished Annie and Jeanette were here with the car, in case they had to get Robyn to a doctor.

"We smell smoke," Alex repeated. "It's making Robyn cough."

"Smoke?" Janie jerked up to a sitting position, sniffing the air. Grabbing the flashlight, she scrambled to her feet. "Alex, help me take a look around. Robyn, make sure everyone stays here until we get back."

"Sure." Robyn's voice was hoarse from coughing. "Like I'd want to go anywhere."

Janie headed for her father's study. "It must be a brush fire. Anything inside the house should have triggered the alarms. I want to see if we can spot something before we decide what to do."

Entering the office was like stepping into an unlit cavern. The windows were sheets of blackness reflecting the weak glow from Janie's flashlight. The wind scraped tree branches against the side of the house, a sound like dozens of small dogs begging to come in at the same time. Janie put out the light and the girls waited for their eyes to adjust. The windows were still dark. The thick clouds blanketed the moon and stars.

After several minutes, Alex thought she saw a faint reddish glow to the north. "What's that?" She took Janie's hand and guided it in the right direction.

"Hmmm." After studying the area, Janie groped her way toward her father's desk. "If I can find my dad's binoculars, we can get a better look."

"Do you want the flashlight?" Alex asked.

"No. Our eyes have adjusted to the dark." A drawer slid open. Janie fumbled inside it. "If we use the light, it will take even longer to see if there's something out there.''

Alex studied the telltale glow. It was impossible to judge distances in the dark, but something that small must be a long way from here. She wondered how far somebody could see from this window on a clear day.

"Found them!" Janie unsnapped the top and slid the binoculars out of the case. "Where are you, Alex? I don't want to stumble over something and break them.''

"I'm right here. All you have to do is walk straight toward the sound of my voice.'' Alex crossed her fingers, hoping that she hadn't forgotten anything that might trip Janie.

Janie shuffled toward her, moving slowly to keep her balance. When she reached Alex, Janie pressed the binoculars into her hands. "Here. Since you spotted it, you try first. Your night vision must be better than mine.''

The binoculars were big and heavy, much larger than any Alex had ever used. She put the strap over her neck so she wouldn't drop them. Janie had removed the lens caps. Alex braced herself against the window frame and looked through the eyepieces. "These things are huge. What does your dad use them for?''

"He got them to look at the stars, but he hasn't been doing any astronomy lately." Janie shifted position, her feet shuffling on the rug.

At first Alex couldn't see anything. The dark night and the lack of identifiable objects made it difficult to locate anything and impossible to focus the lenses. That made searching a slow and frustrating process. Even though she knew the general direction she had been looking, Alex needed several minutes before she finally panned across the right area. She gasped.

It *was* a fire, and it looked like it was going to be a big one. It was behind a long, massive ridge that jutted out from the mountains. *That would be Surveyor's Ridge*, Alex thought, remembering how it dominated the area. The ridge was silhouetted against the red-orange blaze in the canyon behind it. Several tongues of fire had spilled over the crest of the ridge and were racing across the adjacent hillsides.

"We have a problem." Alex handed the binoculars to Janie. "The canyon behind Surveyor's Ridge is burning. The fire is coming our way."

Janie adjusted the binoculars. "You're right. That's several miles north of us, but I don't like the way it's moving. Why don't you call your parents?"

Alex fumbled for the flashlight. It went on, flickered, then steadied to a feeble glow. She could barely see the phone wedged between the baskets of papers on Mr. Robertson's desk.

She picked up the receiver. Silence greeted her. Clicking the switch several times did no good. The line was dead. Alex hung up the phone. "We have a big problem. The phones are out."

Janie took a deep breath. "We'd better tell the others. This *isn't* what I had in mind for the weekend."

"Do you have a bike or something we could use to ride down to the neighbors' to get help?"

"Jeanette borrowed my bike last weekend." Janie shook her head tiredly. "Now it's in even worse shape than hers."

When they joined the others, everyone was stirring. Alex found the other flashlight and turned it on. She hoped there were more batteries somewhere in the house, because these were wearing out.

"All right, everybody," Janie announced with more confidence than she had shown to Alex a few minutes earlier. "We have a small problem on our hands."

"What's the matter?" Nicole mumbled, rubbing her eyes sleepily. "Is the house burning down?"

"No," Alex answered, "but the thunderstorm appears to have started a major fire in the mountains."

"What?" Nicole snapped awake. "You're kidding, aren't you?"

"How bad?" Talking made Robyn start coughing again.

"The main fire is still on the far side of Surveyor's Ridge," Alex said. "The bad news is the wind's blowing it this way."

"You *have* called someone to come get us, haven't you?" Laura asked. "I mean, this is the sort of emergency that we needed Jeanette and her car for. And where is she?"

Janie shook her head. *"That's* our other problem. Alex tried to call her parents, but the phone is out. We're on our own until someone finds us."

Irina scrambled into her jeans. "It is stupid to wait for the fire to come here. I am walking to town now."

Tanya shook her head. "That's not a good idea. The road down the canyon heads north, straight toward the fire."

"I do not need the road." Irina tied a bandanna around her hair. "I can cut straight for town."

"That's a bad idea," Laura said. "You'd be completely unprotected if the fire jumps the canyon. Also, no one will know where to look for you. If you get lost, it could be days before you're found."

"That's right," Alex said. "If this area is in danger, the sheriff's department will evacuate the houses. If we leave, no one will know where to look for us."

Irina's mouth compressed into a hard line, but she didn't say anything. Alex was afraid they hadn't convinced her to stay.

"My uncle works for the Forest Service." Nicole looked straight at Irina. "He says, when you're fighting a fire and it comes toward you, you *don't* run. You find the lowest spot around and dig a hole to hide in. And you *stay put* until the fire passes."

"Just let it burn right over you?" Tanya shuddered. "I don't like that idea *at all.*"

Inspiration hit Alex. She *knew* what to say to convince Irina. After all, Annie had suggested the idea hours ago. "We've got the swimming pool. It's a big hole, and it's already filled with water. If we don't get rescued first, the pool is absolutely the safest place we could be."

One by one, the other girls nodded. Irina was the last, but finally she agreed to stay. Alex hoped she was right. After all, it was odd that her father hadn't already showed up to take them into town. She had expected Annie to call when Mr. and Mrs. Mack got home. They'd never want her to stay out there with no phone. If the phone was out then, Alex knew her parents would have driven out to get the girls immediately. *Unless something's seriously wrong . . .*

Janie jumped to her feet, grabbing the flashlight. "I'm going to soak down the roof. I doubt that anything will happen, but I can't stand sitting here doing nothing."

"And how will you see to do that?" Robyn coughed again. "I wouldn't trust that flashlight to walk down the hall."

"Don't worry," Laura said. "Uncle Ben has some *serious* emergency equipment in the garage."

"Then count me in. I don't feel like sitting around, either." Alex shoved her feet into her shoes.

"Let Robyn be the equipment manager," Nicole suggested around another fit of Robyn's coughing. "The rest of us can do the more energetic stuff."

Robyn's face looked paler than usual, but she didn't argue with Nicole. Alex nodded to herself. There was very little chance they were in any real danger, but doing nothing made things seem more scary. Helping Janie was a whole lot better than worrying about what might happen.

"Then we're agreed." Janie waited for the others to get dressed. "We'll soak down the roof and everything close to the house. That way, if any sparks blow this way, we'll be safe until someone shows up to get us out of here."

"Annie, I'm very disappointed in you." Mr. Mack's mouth was set in a grim line. "You promised to be available in case your sister or her friends needed you. Why did you run off with the only car available, leaving them completely on their own?"

Annie squeezed her eyes shut. Her dad wasn't saying anything she hadn't already told herself a dozen times since Jeanette insisted on driving into town. That didn't make it any easier. "I'm sorry, Dad. We really shouldn't have left."

"What's wrong with us driving into town to

rent a video and get the notes Annie forgot?" Jeanette protested.

"Jeanette!" Annie glared at her friend. "You know it all when it comes to calculus, but you're dead wrong here. We never should have left them without a car."

"How was I supposed to know the lightning was going to start a fire? That tonight was going to be the test of our practice fire drill and evacuation?" Jeanette turned her back to Annie.

Annie reached for her shoulder, then dropped her hand. There was no point continuing the argument. Jeanette was viewing this fire as just another of her father's safety tests. Unless she faced a direct threat, Jeanette wouldn't change her mind.

"What can I do to help, Dad?" she asked.

Mr. Mack glanced toward the television. The local station was showing pictures of the brush fire in the hills north of town. The same footage had been repeating for the last two hours. "I'll go get your sister and her friends," he said. "You keep trying to get through on the phone to tell them I'm coming. Also, call the other parents so they don't worry."

"Right, Dad." Annie dialed the Robertsons'

number. She got a busy signal, as she had for the last hour. That worried her. This late, even Alex's friends were usually in bed. It made no sense that the girls would be on the phone. Annie was beginning to wonder if something was wrong at the Robertsons' house.

CHAPTER 6

Laura had been right about the emergency equipment, Alex thought as Janie and her cousin opened the boxes. The small garage attached to the house had been converted to storage. Rows of shelves, stacked with boxes of food and equipment, filled the space. There were strap-on cleats for their shoes, climbing ropes, safety belts, hard hats with miner's lamps, and many items she couldn't recognize. Several shovels stood next to a shelf that held enough hoses to stock a medium-size store.

"Our biggest problem is that there aren't enough good lights to go around," Janie said. "Dad bought three new ones last spring, and they work great. But everyone else will have to use the old ones."

"That's all right," Laura said. "You're not getting me up on that roof for anything. Not even with floodlights and a movie crew."

"I thought we agreed that everyone was going to help soak things down," Nicole said. "What are you planning to do, then?"

Laura shrugged. "Anything, as long as I can keep both feet on solid ground. I get dizzy if I have to stand on the second rung of a ladder."

"This is stupid." Irina scowled at Laura. "The roof needs to be wet, so all should help do the job. We should not stand here and argue over who gets out of doing the work."

"As I recall, I was drafted as equipment manager." Robyn's words were punctuated by coughs. "If Laura won't go up on the roof, she gets one of the older lamps. She can soak down the trees and grass on the north side of the house."

Janie strapped a wide leather belt around her waist and clipped a rope to the loop. "I'm going up on the roof, but Robyn is right. Most of you should soak down the trees and grass around the house."

Alex thought for a moment. Climbing around

on the roof, even with cleats and a safety line, wasn't her idea of fun. On the other hand, it would give her a good view of the situation. With luck, she might be able to use her powers to help get them rescued. "I'll help you soak down the roof."

Janie's face relaxed into a grin of relief. "Good. If we can get someone to help us with the ladder and keep our hoses from getting caught, everyone else can stay on the ground."

"I'll do it," Nicole said. "I don't mind climbing on a ladder, if I have to. You might need someone who can get up on the roof with you."

Robyn started handing out the equipment—cleats and new lamps for Alex and Janie, older lamps for the others. A sketchy map that Laura found in a box of spray nozzles for the hoses showed where the faucets were. Janie divided the area around the house into zones, based on the length of the hoses.

In the bottom of a box, Alex discovered a carton of industrial-grade dust masks. Robyn grabbed one and fitted it over her face before handing out the others to everybody else. Alex put hers on, molding the metal strip to the shape of her nose and positioning the rubber straps behind her head. It felt like she was breathing through a heavy blanket, but the mask got rid of most of the smoke. Even Robyn quit coughing so much.

"All right, guys. We all know what we're doing." Janie picked up one end of the ladder. Nicole took the other. Alex wrestled a large coil of hose onto her shoulder and staggered after them. It would have been easy to move all the hoses with her powers, but she couldn't do it without being caught. She'd have to keep her eyes open for a way to use the cover of darkness to help them.

While Janie and Nicole positioned the ladder, Alex hooked up the hose and went back for another. Everyone was outside, so she floated the longest hose off the shelf and onto her shoulder. Using her powers to support the weight, Alex guided the hose to the faucet closest to her section of the roof. She screwed the end to the faucet and rejoined Janie and Nicole.

By then, they had the ladder in place. Janie showed Alex how to fasten the sawtoothed metal cleats onto her shoes, then started up the ladder. Alex watched her climb, thinking, *What have I gotten myself into this time?*

George Mack slowed the car to avoid hitting the pickup ahead of him. He had been driving too fast, he knew, but it still annoyed him that the other driver was slowing. Brake lights flared, and the truck stopped. Mr. Mack slammed on his own brakes. Ahead of the pickup, he saw flashing amber lights on a barricade. Beyond it, a police car was parked across the pavement. The highway was closed.

A uniformed officer walked over to the truck. After a brief conversation, the deputy stepped back. The pickup made a U-turn and headed back for Paradise Valley.

Mr. Mack inched forward until he was even with the officer. She came over. "I'm sorry, sir. The road is closed to everything but emergency vehicles because of the fire."

"But my daughter is staying with some friends who live in Pedregoso Canyon. I was just going to pick her up."

The deputy shook her head. "Everyone has been evacuated from the canyons already. Your daughter and her friends should have been taken to one of the evacuation centers."

"How long ago was that?" Fear and annoyance made Mr. Mack's voice sharper than he had intended. Alex would have called home if she was safe. "My other daughter has been trying to phone her sister for the last two hours. Without any luck."

"I'm not surprised. The electricity and phones have been out in that area all evening." The deputy rubbed a hand across her eyes. "Pedregoso Canyon was the last area to be evacuated. By the time you get home, your daughter should be there."

Mr. Mack gave the officer his most appealing smile. "It's only another five miles to her friend's house. I really should check to see that the girls didn't get overlooked."

"I can't allow you to do that, sir. The sheriff's office has a checklist to make sure they get everyone." The officer reached for her ticket book. "If you don't head back for town now, I'll have to write you up for blocking the road for emergency vehicles and failure to obey my instructions."

Mr. Mack permitted himself a brief fantasy of crashing through the barricade to rescue the girls. It wouldn't work. "That won't be necessary," he told the officer reluctantly. She stepped away, and he turned the car around.

As he headed back to Paradise Valley, he kept replaying the scene in his mind. Despite the deputy's assurances, he had no proof the girls had been evacuated. *I should have tried harder*, he thought. He should have insisted on making sure that Alex and her friends were safe. With the phone out, the girls had no way to let anyone know if they had been missed by the rescue teams.

Although Alex hadn't been overly worried about keeping her balance on the sloping roof, moving around was easier than she had expected. The cleats bit into the shingles, making it almost impossible to slip. The safety line, which clipped to her belt and tied to an eyebolt, prevented her from falling farther than the length of the rope. The eyebolts had been installed as anchors at ten-foot intervals along the ridge of the roof. With a little practice, she found she could lean her weight against the rope and use the eyebolt as a pivot to move quickly from one side of the roof to the other.

Even so, the view from the roof was scary. Alex swallowed nervously. She was two stories above the ground, and her powers wouldn't save her from a fall. Not that she believed the fire would get so close as to threaten her position.

At the far end of the house, Janie's light bobbed back and forth as she soaked the shingles within reach of her hose. On the ground below, shafts of light showed where her friends were working. Up here, Alex was all alone.

She moved to the base of the tower and braced herself against the wall. After studying the area so she knew where to point her spray nozzle, Alex switched off her light. For a moment, the darkness was terrifying. She let her eyes adjust, and she began to see shapes in the surrounding night.

To the north, Alex had no trouble seeing the fire, even without the binoculars. The scarlet glow had spilled over Surveyor's Ridge and was spreading across the hills at an alarming rate. She couldn't see any details, but her imagination supplied them. Briefly, she wished the special powers she'd developed after being accidentally doused in GC-161 included telescopic vision so she could see what was happening.

The growl of a heavy, slow-moving airplane rolled over the house. Alex looked up, searching for the plane. From the sound, it had to be almost directly overhead, but she could see nothing. The smoke overhead was too thick. Then, in a brief gap in the smoke, she spotted the plane's running lights.

Alex checked the locations of her friends. Judging from the angle of her light, Janie's back was toward her. She could see one light on the ground, also pointing away from her. The other girls were out of sight.

Crossing her fingers, Alex shot a zapper to one side of the plane's flight path. She wanted to get the pilot's attention, wanted him to think someone on the ground was sending up flares. However, she did *not* want to hit the plane. She wasn't sure what a zapper would do to it. Finding out, even by accident, wasn't going to help get them rescued.

The smoke closed in around the plane, and the drone of its engines continued on course for the fire. Alex wished she knew if her impromptu flare had been seen. She tracked the sounds, trying to guess where to send a second zapper.

A light peeked over the edge of the roof. "Alex! Alex, where are you?" Nicole called.

Alex switched her light back on. "Over here, Nicole."

"I couldn't see your light. I was worried something had happened to you." Nicole moved cautiously toward her.

"I didn't mean to worry you. I turned off my light so I could see the fire. It's spreading awfully fast." Alex pointed her light at the shingles, checking for any spots she had missed. Even in the dark, she had done a thorough job of soaking things.

Nicole stopped beside her, leaning against the tower wall. Her filter mask was a bright oval against her dark skin. "Janie said the same thing. She's not sure we'll be able to keep things wet enough to do any good."

Alex swept her light in an arc. Tree branches leaped into sinister outlines against the smoke-filled blackness. If the fire came their way, the trees were too close to the house. "I wish those trees weren't there," she murmured.

"Yeah," Nicole agreed. "As dry as everything is, they'll go up like torches."

Alex gave the trees another look. This time, they seemed more threatening and the danger from the fire more real. She drew in a deep breath. "I don't want to worry you or anything, Nicole. But I think we're in a lot of trouble."

"So that's as far as I got," George Mack said, shaking his head. "The officer at the roadblock insisted that everyone had been evacuated from the houses in the canyon." As Annie and her mother listened to his story, identical worried frowns gathered on their faces. The faces of the other parents, clustered around the Macks, alternated between concern and anger.

"I don't like this," Barbara Mack said. "Alex should have called us. There isn't enough room in the evacuation centers. A lot of those people don't have any place to go. They'd want anyone who could to stay with friends or family."

Annie looked from one parent to the other. "How are we going to find them?"

"Let's see." Mr. Mack counted off the points he was making on his fingers. "We can try calling all the centers, but they're probably swamped with phone calls already. That is, assuming they have someone to answer the phones at this hour. I wish there was some way we could check the Robertsons' house."

"I'll ask Ray to try calling," Annie suggested. "He'll want to help, and that won't tie up our phone if Alex tries to call here." Several of the other parents offered to make phone calls from their offices.

"Good idea," Mr. Mack said. "We'll need someone here at the house in case Alex calls in. And the rest of us can check the evacuation centers."

"Jeanette can handle the phone," Annie said. "That way I can check the nearby schools—

they're the closest evac centers. You guys can drive to the more distant ones. No telling where they'll take them."

"Are you sure you want to be out riding your bike at this hour?" Mrs. Mack asked.

Annie shook her head. "Don't worry, Mom. It takes all of fifteen minutes to ride from the junior high to the high school, then to the elementary school and home. I'll be back in an hour. An hour and a half, tops—depending on how long it takes to see if Alex is there."

Mrs. Mack frowned. "I don't like it, but it would let the rest of us concentrate on the places that are farther away."

"Then it's settled," Mr. Mack said. "Annie will take the schools in the neighborhood. Barbara, do we have a map we can use to lay out search areas for the rest of us?"

Mrs. Mack nodded and went to fetch the map. Mr. Wong, Tanya's father, spoke up. "I have a pilot's license. As soon as it's light, I'll check the house to see if they're still there."

The idea was met with cheers from the other parents and offers to help rent the plane. Mr. Mack grinned with relief. "That solves that problem. Until then, the search teams will report back to Jeanette every half hour. Annie, when you've checked the schools, come home and take over the phone duties."

"But, Dad—"

"No 'buts,' Annie." He gave her a stern look. "At this hour of the night, drivers aren't looking for bicyclists. That makes it too easy for you to get in an accident. Besides, I'd rather you handled the phone."

Annie glanced into the living room. After insisting that her sister knew what to do in an emergency, Jeanette had gone back to searching for something to watch on TV. *As if the fire is no more real than a TV show*, Annie thought, realizing why Jeanette's attitude bothered her. Her father was right. Maybe Alex and her friends could take care of themselves, but Annie wanted to know they were safe. "I'll get back as fast as I can, Dad."

"All right, team." Mr. Mack reached for his keys. "Let's get moving. We've got a lot of ground to cover."

CHAPTER 7

Around four in the morning, Robyn called them inside for drinks and food. A battery-powered lantern cast a circle of light just big enough to cover the kitchen table. "We better drink the milk before it spoils," she said, pointing to the milk and cereal she had laid out. "Everybody's working hard, and you need to eat."

"I just want to sleep." Laura moaned and buried her face in her hands. "I never realized this place was so big."

"Sleep would be good." Tanya nibbled her cereal listlessly. Her face was sweat streaked and dirt smudged, except for where her mask had been. "But I suppose someone is going to insist that we stay up all night just for the fun of it."

"I wasn't going to mention it," Nicole said, "but I think the wind was changing direction when we came inside."

"What direction was it changing to?" Even as she asked, Alex had a feeling she wouldn't like the answer.

"Toward us?" Robyn asked. "I'll bet it was starting to blow the fire straight toward us."

A chorus of groans greeted Nicole's nod. "That's what it felt like," she said. "We'd better keep an eye on it."

"Then everybody eat up," Janie said. "Because the wind usually picks up just before dawn."

"Some party," Tanya muttered, pouring herself another glass of milk. "Are we having fun yet?"

"Of course we are!" Laura gave her best friend the phony grin she used when her mother gave her extra chores. "The entire school will be pea green with envy at our unique experience."

"Isn't that the truth!" Nicole's tone dripped with sarcasm.

The comments are getting a little nasty, Alex thought. She glanced toward Janie, who was slumped in her chair. "Is something wrong?" Alex asked.

Janie shrugged, her movements slow and stiff. "This isn't what I had in mind when I invited everybody to a slumber party."

"It's not your fault." Alex forced a weak smile. "Besides, we *will* have a wild story to tell once this is over."

Janie straightened a little in her chair. "Even if things are a bit too 'interesting' right now?"

"That's what makes a great story." Alex crossed her fingers, hoping they would get to tell their tale. When the fire had been miles away and the wind wasn't blowing toward them, the danger hadn't been real. Now, however, it looked like they could get caught by the fire. Why hadn't someone rescued them? Her father should have been here hours ago. What had happened?

"What do you mean—everyone from that area was evacuated before midnight?" George Mack leaned over the counter to glare at the young dispatcher. In the background, the murmur of voices and the crackle of radio chatter filled the room. "How do you know? The house is at the far end of the canyon."

The dispatcher ruffled through the pages on his clipboard. "Pedregoso Canyon was one of the last areas evacuated, but we had everybody out before midnight. Have you checked at Atron Junior High? That's where the people from that area were taken."

Mr. Mack slammed his fist against the counter. "Yes, we've checked Atron Junior High! My oldest daughter checked two hours ago. The girls weren't there."

"I don't know." The dispatcher flipped through his lists again. "All I know is that the Robertson house is marked off and everyone from Pedregoso Canyon was taken to Atron Junior High. I suggest you try again. They'll have a list of everyone there."

The phone rang, and the young man turned to answer it. Mr. Mack grabbed for the clipboard and ruffled through the pages. There were check marks beside all the houses in Pedregoso Canyon.

Frustrated, Mr. Mack slammed down the clipboard and stormed out. If Alex and her friends had been taken to the junior high, they'd be at the Mack house by now. Maybe someone at the junior high knew where they were.

*   *   *

After a few minutes the conversation around the table lagged. One by one, the girls dozed off.

Alex's arms and shoulders ached from holding the hose for so long, and her hands hurt from squeezing the pistol grip on the spray nozzle. Her throat was raw from breathing the smoke, even through the mask. She felt like her head was stuffed with cotton and her brain replaced with lumpy oatmeal. More than anything, she wanted to be at home in her own bed, sound asleep. She fumbled her mask into place before she completely faded out.

The snap of windblown fabric roused Alex. She rubbed her eyes and looked around, trying to remember where she was. Slowly, as if through a thick haze, the details came back. She adjusted her mask, which had slipped sideways while she slept.

Irina straightened, rubbing smoke-reddened eyes. "What is making that noise?"

Alex frowned, trying to identify the sound. It was coming from right outside the door. "I think the wind is blowing the awning. It sounds awfully loud."

Their voices disturbed the others. One by one, the girls struggled awake.

"This is what I was afraid of," Janie said. "The

wind sounds strong enough to blow the fire right to us."

"Let's check from upstairs before we go out," Alex suggested. "I'd like to see what we're up against."

"Me, too," echoed the others.

"Good idea." Janie led them to her father's office. Her flashlight gave only a feeble light, its batteries starting to fail. Alex thought the smoke smelled stronger as they climbed.

"Uh, Janie—I hate to bring this up," Laura said with a question in her voice, "but shouldn't the smoke detectors have gone off with this much junk in the air?"

"I don't know." Janie opened the door to the office. "Unless Mom forgot to replace the batteries."

"Or she reduced the sensitivity so the alarm wouldn't go off while she's cooking," Laura suggested.

"There is that."

Good thing Nicole is too sleepy to comment on the importance of responsibility, Alex thought grimly.

After the dark stairwell, Alex had no trouble finding her way across the office. The hills to the north and east of the canyon were ablaze. The ruddy glow was bright enough to see by.

The wind had driven rivers of flame across the brushy hills. The leading edge was well south of the highway. *It's so close,* Alex thought. *Probably less than a mile away.* Wind-tossed sparks ignited fires ahead of the main blaze. These blossomed into large splotches of red on the dark hillside. Higher up the mountains to the north and east, the inferno raged unchecked.

Laura asked, "Janie, have I ever told you the view from this window is a bit much?"

"That fire is *way* too close for comfort," Tanya said.

"It won't be easy." Alex fumbled to put her skittering thoughts into words. "If we all pitch in, maybe we can keep the fire away from the house. We've got a good start. We just have to keep soaking the ground around the house as well."

Nicole started for the door. "I'm game. If we're stranded out here, it only makes sense to protect our shelter."

Irina shook her head. "I do not suppose this is a good time to mention that tile roofs do not burn."

The other girls groaned. Alex followed Nicole from the room. "If the water holds up and we can keep the sparks from igniting anything nearby, we *can* do it."

Another chorus of groans greeted Alex's statement. That didn't change the facts. After the previous few hours, the last thing Alex wanted to do was to get up on the roof again. She wiped her sweaty palms on her jeans. All her earlier work would be wasted if she gave up now. The other girls knew that, too. They followed as she and Nicole headed outside.

Alex strapped on her safety equipment and climbed back up on the roof. A quick look around showed several patches where the wind had already dried the shingles. She moved the hose into position, using her powers to help lift it, and began wetting things down. Luckily, most of the roof was still damp.

"I can handle this end of things for a while," she called to the others. From her vantage point, she could see the fire clearly. Glowing bits of grass swirled in the air. Alex's eyes watered and her throat burned from the smoke. She pinched her mask tighter around her nose, wondering if it was still working.

The wind was blowing in gusts, one moment still and the next whipping the flames toward the rim of the canyon. With a start, Alex realized how very low the walls were. From the roof of the Robertsons' house, she could see the hills above the rim.

"The wind is blowing sparks into the grass behind the gazebo," Alex called to the others.

"Can you spot for us?" Janie shouted up to her.

"No problem." A sudden downdraft carried a swarm of glowing pinpoints into a patch of dry grass near the canyon wall. "There's a spot straight behind the gazebo, over near the rocks, that's starting to burn."

"Quick! Put the hoses together and relay them out there," Janie ordered. She disappeared into the garage and, moments later, staggered out with a large coil of hose. Alex reached out with her powers, supporting some of the weight so Janie could move faster. She could have moved the hose, but that would have alerted the other girls that something strange was happening.

Janie reached the end of the hose Irina had been using earlier. She dropped her load, removed the spray nozzle, and screwed the two hoses together. With the free end in her hand, she jogged toward the fire. "Somebody bring another hose!"

Two more blazes had started from windblown sparks by the time Laura arrived with the next hose. Alex checked the location of the other girls, but no one could reach those fires in time.

How far away are the fires? Alex wondered. She wasn't sure she could control her telekinesis at that distance, but she had to try. Otherwise, they would have three grass fires behind the house, and only one hose in position to fight them.

She spotted a patch of bare dirt and gravel near the cliffs. Concentrating hard, she scooped up handful-sized globs of dirt and threw them onto the largest grass fire.

At first, this made things worse by stirring up air currents and fanning the flames. Alex experimented, discovering that working from several directions kept the fire contained. She threw dirt on the flames until she smothered them.

"Water!" Janie yelled. Irina and Tanya, who were carrying the hose to the other fire, echoed the call. Distracted by the shout, Alex jumped. Her load of dirt fell short of its target.

Laura turned on the faucet, but Janie again shouted for water. The stream from Alex's hose dropped to a trickle. With all the hoses running, the pressure was dropping. *The water isn't going to reach the end of Janie's long hose,* Alex thought.

She focused her powers on the water pipes. With great effort, Alex lifted the water, forcing more of it through the squirming, twisting hose. Janie fought to keep the end pointed toward the fire. The water sprayed out, drenching the flames. The fire sputtered, flickered, and finally went out.

A ragged cheer went up from Janie and her helpers. As Alex looked toward Laura's group, a cloud of sparks and hot debris settled behind the garage. "The shed!" Alex screamed as the old shingles caught fire.

Janie raced for the shed, dragging her hose behind her. It wasn't going to be enough, Alex realized. The flames were faster than Janie's crew. It would take all the hoses to keep the fire from spreading to the garage.

Hoping no one was watching, Alex morphed and slid down the house. She returned to human form and dashed for the shed, using her powers to haul the hose after her.

By the time she got there, the shed was encased in flame. Greedy tentacles of yellow and orange twisted through the blackening boards. Alex turned her hose on the shed. If they couldn't stop the fire here, it would spread to the garage. The water hissed and spit as it hit the flames, sending up clouds of smoke, steam, and more sparks. Using her powers, Alex lifted more water onto the shed, but she wasn't sure she was doing any good. She was so tired her legs were starting to shake.

The shed collapsed, scattering sparks and burning wreckage. The girls pounced on the fiery debris with hoses and shovels. A cloud of sparks landed on Alex's arm, biting at her skin like vicious insects until she swatted them.

Finally the fire was out. Alex started back for the house, wondering if she had enough strength left to climb back up on the roof. From the west, the drone of a slow-moving airplane rolled over the landscape. It was flying close to the ground. Alex looked for it, but the smoke overhead was too thick.

Hoping for the best, she tried to send a zapper to one side of its course. Nothing happened. She tried again, and a slight flicker danced around her fingertips. After her recent efforts, she was too exhausted to get a signal off.

The plane continued on course. *What's going to happen to me and my friends?* she wondered. *How can I make someone notice us, especially if my powers aren't working?*

CHAPTER 8

The drone of the plane's engines faded as it headed north toward the heart of the fire. Alex slumped in defeat. What good were her powers, if they abandoned her when she desperately *needed* to attract attention with them? Tiredly, she crawled back up onto the roof, dragging her hose with her.

The wind swirled a cloud of sparks toward her. They settled like fireflies on the far end of the roof. There were a couple of dry patches down there that she hadn't soaked earlier, Alex remembered with a sinking feeling in her stomach. If the sparks landed in those areas, they would set the shingles afire unless she got them out quickly.

She needed to get to the other end of the roof fast, but her safety line would not reach that far. Alex unclipped it and wrapped the line around her waist. Hoping her cleats would do their job, she hurried along the ridge line. She *had* to protect the house.

As tired as she was, it wasn't easy to keep her balance in the smoky darkness while dragging the hose. She slipped once, falling to her knees and dropping the hose. After that, she used her powers to pull it after her so she could use her arms for balance. It was a struggle, but adrenaline was starting to give her the energy she needed.

By the time she reached her goal, most of the sparks had sputtered out. A few larger fragments of debris still smoldered, and wisps of smoke rose from one patch of shingles. Alex pointed the hose at it and used her telekinetic powers to pull the water through the hose faster. She couldn't allow the fire to take hold.

The water drenched the burning patch and washed the sparks off the roof. When she was sure the immediate danger was over, Alex paused to clip her safety line to the nearest eyebolt. While she was there, she might as well soak these dry spots.

"Over here!" Nicole yelled.

"I see it," Laura shouted back. "We're coming."

Alex looked for Nicole, finally spotting her light behind the ruined shed. Another patch of dry grass had caught fire. The flames were spreading toward the trees surrounding the house. It would be close. Alex couldn't tell whether the fire would reach the trees before Laura got the hose into position.

She couldn't let the flames reach the trees. If they did, they couldn't keep the house from burning. She had to slow it down until Laura got there. Hoping Nicole couldn't see what she was doing, Alex dumped a pile of dirt on the leading edge of the fire.

"Ouch!" Nicole threw up her arm to protect her eyes from the dust. Alex tossed more dirt on the flames.

Laura charged up, blasting at the fire with the hose. To Alex's relief, the scarlet flames quickly melted to smoky, flickering embers. The fire went out, still far enough away from the trees.

A shout from the opposite side of the house sent Janie and her team to put out another fire. Alex tried to help, but more sparks settled on the roof. Suddenly she had more work than even she could handle.

Even using her powers to move the hose, Alex was kept running for the next hour. The fire was like an evil spirit that took perverse delight in showing Alex how insignificant her efforts were. Every time she put out one batch of sparks, two more landed—one at each end of the house.

A gust of wind hit the house, eddied around the tower, and dumped its load of sparks on the roof. The airflow patterns around the house were sending a triple share of sparks her way. Even so, to keep ahead of the fire, she needed her powers to throw water on the sparks she couldn't reach in time. She hoped no one was watching her.

Alex was finally making progress when Janie's head appeared above the eaves. "How's it going?"

She could see Janie, Alex realized with a start. Sometime in the last hour, while she had been too busy to notice, the sky had started to lighten to a thick, smoky gray. "It's going," Alex replied. A longer answer seemed like too much trouble. Somewhere in the smoke, a small plane droned over the house.

Janie hauled herself onto the roof. She was

dragging a hose. "I think we've won this round. The wind has changed direction. It's blowing the fire away from us."

"Is it?" Alex tried to tell where the wind was coming from, but it was too much work. She was too tired to care. "I guess so."

"We should give the roof one more soaking, then try to get some rest," Janie said. "There's no telling how long a break we'll get."

"Sounds good to me."

Alex started near the tower, while Janie took the other end. On the ground, the other girls coiled the hoses and stacked them by the faucets. Irina and Tanya, shovels in hand, patrolled the area between the cliffs and the main buildings. They were looking for any smoldering patches they had missed earlier. A little dirt could do the job just as well as water in that case.

Everyone finished at the same time. The others gathered near the ladder. Janie shouted for someone to turn off the water and pull her hose down. It slithered over the edge.

Janie stepped on the ladder. Her foot slipped, pushing the ladder away from the house. She grabbed for the gutter but missed. The ladder tilted farther away. Janie screamed in panic.

*　　*　　*

Mr. Mack whipped the car into the junior high parking lot, sliding a little as he completed the turn. He parked the car across two spots and jumped out. Mrs. Mack and Annie followed him. Annie shook her head. "I already checked here, Dad. No one had seen them."

"This is where they were *supposed* to be taken." His long strides covered the ground swiftly. "That means we ask everyone here until we get a straight answer."

Annie glanced around. It was strange to see the parking lot and school yard so full of activity at this hour. Several pickups and a van from the plant were unloading food and bedding at the door to the gym. The cars near the door probably belonged to the people running the evacuation center. A dozen other vehicles, scattered around the lot and parked at odd angles, suggested others were looking for missing friends and family.

As she jogged across the lawn, Annie thought the smoke was thicker than it had been earlier. Did that mean the fire was getting closer? Planes droned overhead, passing back and forth from the Paradise Valley airport. Most of them, she guessed, were carrying chemicals to drop on the fire. One of them should be Mr. Wong's small plane. Would he be able to see Alex and her friends through the thick smoke?

Inside the gym was a makeshift command post. A bronze-skinned, balding man was sitting behind the paper-strewn table, checking off items on a clipboard. "What do you want?" he demanded. Looking up from his list, a smile lit his face. "George! Am I glad to see you! Can we ever use your help!"

"Actually, that's not why I'm here, Ricardo," Mr. Mack said. He tried to remember which section of the plant Ricardo worked in. "I'm looking for my daughter and some friends. They were out at the Robertsons' in Pedregoso Canyon for the weekend."

"The Robertsons? In Pedregoso Canyon?" Ricardo reached for another clipboard and ruffled through the pages. "It says they were accounted for by the evacuation teams."

"Then the girls are here?"

Ricardo looked back at the paper. "They should be . . . that's funny. The house is checked off, but there aren't any names here. This isn't right."

Mr. Mack reached for the clipboard, read the notes, and handed it back. "Do you mind if we ask around a bit? We've been trying to locate the girls for the last six hours."

"Be my guest. But I could sure use some help."

A young man parked a hand truck stacked with boxes beside the table. He dumped a pile of forms in front of Ricardo, who grabbed the papers. Ricardo signed the top one and returned it to the delivery man. Wrestling his hand truck free of the boxes, the young man left.

"I see what you mean," Mr. Mack said. "We'll call Mr. Alvarado to come over, and I'll give you a hand as soon as we find my daughter and her friends."

The Macks split up and moved among the people in the gym. Many of the people were trying to sleep, leaning against the wall or curled up on blankets. Still, enough people were awake to make questioning them a daunting task.

Looking around, Annie realized she hadn't seen so many people in the gym since the playoff game with Pittsville Gardens her first year at the junior high. When Atron's team lost, she promised herself never again to waste her time on such trivial pursuits. That memory brought home the size of the task facing them.

She picked her way through the bleachers,

asking for the people who lived in Pedregoso Canyon. She *had* to find Alex. If she didn't, she'd never be able to face her parents—or herself—for letting Jeanette talk her into going to town on such a silly errand.

After almost an hour, Annie found someone who lived in Pedregoso Canyon. Toby Hoover was a friend of Jeanette's older brother. "No, the rescue squad didn't go up there," Toby said. "Jimmy said his family was going to the lake for the weekend. When I saw Jeanette's car headed for town, I knew there wasn't anyone up there."

"What do you mean? Didn't they check the house anyway?" Annie's stomach clenched into a hard knot.

Toby shrugged, but a shrill tone slipped into his voice. "Why bother? Since no one was up there, I told them we'd already checked. The deputies were running behind schedule. Everybody had to get out of the canyon before the fire got there."

"You mean, you wanted them to get *you* out as fast as possible. Without checking on everyone else," Annie said in a flat voice. Underneath her controlled exterior, her temper flared. What right did he have to assume that no one was at the Robertsons'?

Toby shrugged again, but his voice rose higher. "They asked. I told them what I knew. How was I to know someone was still up there?"

Annie bit back an angry reply. Fighting with Toby over his selfish mistake wouldn't help Alex and her friends. She turned away. Halfway down the stairs, she saw her father looking toward her. She signaled frantically for him to join her. They would have to act fast to rescue Alex.

The ladder hovered in a nearly vertical position, threatening to tip over with Janie. Without thinking, Alex grabbed the ladder with her powers. It wobbled for a moment, then settled gently into place against the eaves. Just to be safe, Alex held it there until Janie reached the ground. She was very glad to let Robyn and Nicole brace the ladder while she descended. She wasn't sure she could use her powers and climb down a ladder at the same time.

"Did you see that?" Tanya asked, letting her breath out in a gasp. "It looked like Janie was going to fall over."

"What happened with the ladder, anyway?" Nicole wanted to know as she helped Alex off it. "I thought Janie was a goner."

"Yeah." Tanya frowned. "It looked like the ladder was really falling. Then it seemed like somebody grabbed it and pulled it back against the house."

Alex slid to the ground, shaking. Janie sat a few feet away, looking as wrung out as Alex felt. Between the hard work and the lack of sleep, no one looked much better. But they all had seen her use her powers to keep the ladder from falling. If she didn't stop them, they would talk about the near accident until the story reached the wrong ears.

"What I saw was Janie balanced on the ladder. First it tipped away from the house and then it came back." *That sounds normal enough*, Alex hoped. She rubbed her stinging eyes, adding for extra protection, "Maybe we're seeing things because we're so tired. Or because we're breathing something weird."

"You mean, like the smoke?" Laura asked.

"It's the chemicals they're dumping on the fire," Robyn said. "We should all be wearing gas masks to protect ourselves."

"Gas masks may be the only thing Uncle Ben doesn't have in his garage." Laura scowled. "Doesn't it just figure?"

Janie pushed herself to her feet. "I don't know

about the rest of you, but I'd like to get breakfast and a nap. I'm not sure how long the wind will keep the fire away from us."

That sounds like a good idea, Alex thought. However, she was more than willing to trade breakfast for sleep. Most of the other girls shared her feelings, but Robyn disagreed.

"Everyone *will* eat breakfast," she insisted. "We've all been working hard, and you guys will start acting really weird if you don't get something to eat."

She herded everybody into the kitchen. Bowls, spoons, and boxes of cold cereal were laid out on the table. The girls sat down and took off their grubby masks.

"Everybody, eat up," Robyn ordered. "If the power stays off too much longer, the milk will spoil. Then we'll be in even more trouble than we are now."

"There *is* powdered milk," Laura said with a grimace. "Didn't you see those boxes of emergency food in the garage?"

A chorus of groans answered her. Alex reached for the granola and poured herself a double helping. She wasn't hungry, but she had to replace the energy she had used. The other girls attacked their cereal, and silence settled over the group.

As they finished, Robyn held up a box holding several slips of paper. "I'll take first watch and clean up the kitchen, since I wasn't working as hard as the rest of you. Everybody else, draw straws to see who's next."

"Do we have to?" Tanya asked. "Can't we just all sleep?"

"No!" Irina's jaw clenched. "We must watch for danger. Or pay the price."

Robyn winced, and Alex could see she was struggling to keep from voicing her usual pessimism. Alex squeezed her friend's arm. "If the wind shifts, we need to get back out there. I suggest half-hour watches, since everybody is really tired."

Still grumbling, Tanya pulled her slip of paper from the box. Alex drew next. To her relief, she got the fourth watch. By then, she hoped she would be a little more alert. Right now, she was so tired she could barely drag herself up the stairs. She was asleep the minute she crawled inside her sleeping bag.

CHAPTER 9

The sound of the wind rattling the windows roused Alex. She groaned and pulled her sleeping bag over her head, but she could still hear the noise. She'd never get back to sleep now. She'd been asleep barely an hour.

"I don't know," Janie said. Her voice was low. Alex thought she was probably over by the window. "I don't like the way the wind is picking up."

"Me, either," Nicole replied, keeping her voice down. "Unfortunately, the smoke is way too thick to see anything."

"I suppose we ought to wake the others." Janie sighed. "I was hoping the sheriff would have found us by now."

"I hear you. I've had my fill of firefighting."

Alex pushed herself to a sitting position. Each muscle protested as she moved. She couldn't remember when she had worked so hard or for so long. To make matters worse, it sounded like they were going to be at it again all too soon.

She stretched and looked around the family room. Laura, Tanya, and Irina were still asleep. Their faces were hidden under the folded corners of their sleeping bags, even though the room was warm enough that they had kicked the rest aside. With the electricity off, the temperature inside mirrored the heat outside. It was too hot and sticky to sleep under many covers.

The curtains were closed, blocking the daylight. As she had guessed, Janie and Nicole were across the room, hidden behind the curtains. Robyn was nowhere in sight.

Alex pulled on her clothes and joined the two at the window. "What's happening?"

"That's what we're trying to decide," Nicole said. "The wind is blowing our way again, but the smoke is too thick to see the fire."

"Oh, great." Alex looked outside. As Nicole had said, smoke blanketed everything. The gazebo beyond the pool was a thicker shadow in the dense haze. Alex was glad she was still wearing her filter mask. "What's the plan?"

"Robyn is finding us something to eat," Nicole said. "After that, I don't know."

An airplane droned over the house. Janie looked upward as if hoping to see it. "We'd better water down the roof again. And I'd like to see if there's anything in the garage we can use to signal that we're here."

"I don't know why my dad hasn't come for us," Alex said. "I thought he'd be here the minute he found Annie and Jeanette at our house."

"The roads must be blocked off." Nicole shook her head. "Otherwise my mom would have beat your dad. She *really* wasn't sure about me coming out here for the weekend."

Robyn appeared in the doorway. "Breakfast is served . . . again," she announced. Her voice roused the sleepers. While they dressed, she joined the trio at the window. Alex thought her friend looked a little more stressed than usual, but Nicole's suggestion that Robyn manage things had been inspired. Having to watch out for everyone else kept her focused on the details of their activities rather than the danger of the situation.

"I figure we'd better finish off the milk,"

Robyn said. "After that, it's lunch meat and peanut butter, unless your dad has a camp stove in his survival gear."

"Somewhere. I'm not sure which box it's in." Janie scratched her head. "Or where the fuel is. However, we could use the barbecue, if Mom actually remembered to buy more briquettes after last weekend."

"One more item to look for." Alex ticked them off on her fingers. "A camp stove and fuel. Failing that, briquettes for the barbecue. Canned food to eat, when the fresh stuff spoils because the electricity is off. A way to signal we're still here. More batteries for the flashlights. Is that everything?"

"Annie's rubbing off on you," Nicole said with a laugh. "That's a very thorough list."

By then, the others were dressed. They trooped down to the kitchen. Robyn had laid out the bowls and cereal again, along with a fresh filter mask for each person. Tanya and Laura protested they were tired of eating cereal. "Eat!" Janie snapped. "Who knows when we'll get another chance."

While they were eating, they argued about what needed doing and who would do it. Most of the girls still didn't want to go up onto the roof. To Alex's surprise, Laura was even more determined to stay on the ground than she had been the previous night. "In the daylight," she insisted, "I can see how far down it is. Falling off the ladder isn't a very good idea."

"Probably not." Alex didn't want to spend all day keeping the shingles wet, but the others weren't giving her much choice. "I'm not afraid of heights. I'll do the roof."

"I'll help," Nicole said. "That way Janie can look for stuff in the garage. She has a better idea about what her dad has than I do."

Janie smiled her thanks. "Right now, I'm beginning to see just how much I *don't* know about what my dad has squirreled away. But I do have a better chance of finding things than the rest of you. Dad keeps lecturing us on what he has stashed away. I just have to remember where things are—this time."

"At least you have the stuff," Robyn said. "That's better than ninety percent of the people in this town."

Janie wrinkled her nose. "That's reassuring— I think."

After breakfast, Alex decided to take a walk.

"Do you want company?" Nicole asked. "You

shouldn't be wandering around here by yourself."

Alex shook her head. "I won't go far. I want to look at what's left of the shed, to see how bad it looks in the daylight. I'll stay in sight of the buildings."

"All right." Nicole shook her head for emphasis. "I *don't* want to see that again."

The shed was a pile of charred debris. Alex gave it a brief inspection, then hunted for the track of the grass fire that almost reached the trees. Last night, the fire had seemed huge and threatening. In daylight, it was much smaller— a patch about twenty feet in diameter with a forty-foot streamer pointing toward the trees. The dirt she'd thrown on the fire was clearly visible, if someone knew what to look for. There wasn't much chance that anyone would figure out how she'd done it.

As she studied the burned area, a plane passed overhead. Alex checked that no one was around. The smoke was very thick, but she waited until she saw the plane as a dim shadow. Crossing her fingers, she sent a string of zappers ahead of the plane.

The aircraft continued with no apparent change in its flight. She wasn't sure what she expected, but the lack of response was disappointing. Dragging her feet, Alex started back.

Before she reached the garage, she heard another plane. She waited until the engine noise was almost overhead. The plane was so low that the pilot *had* to see her zappers, she thought. However, this plane also continued on its course.

"Alex!" Nicole sounded worried. "Alex! Are you all right?"

"Coming!" she answered. If she couldn't get anyone's attention with her zappers, she might as well be watering down the roof. There, at least, her efforts were doing some good.

"Look what I found! A radio!" Janie announced as Alex entered the garage.

"And I found the batteries over there." Robyn pointed to a box next to the door.

"Maybe we can pick up the news and find out what's going on," Laura suggested. "I really feel cut off without the TV and the phone."

Janie put new batteries in the radio and searched for a station. Static greeted her efforts. She shook her head in disgust. "Reception's pretty poor out here. Does anybody remember where the news station is?"

"Who listens to that?" Tanya asked.

"My dad, for one," Robyn said. "I think it's around nine-fifty."

"It is nine five two point seven," Irina said. "It is the only station to which my parents will listen."

"Thanks," Janie said. "It doesn't come in very well out here, but it's our best bet for getting news quickly."

She jiggled the dial, creeping slowly through the numbers between 950 and 955. Finally the sound of a man's voice took shape through the static. Janie tweaked the dial a little more and then turned up the volume.

"Once again, our top story is the largest brush fire to sweep the Paradise Valley area in fifty years. Fueled by strong winds and high temperatures, over ten thousand acres have burned since lightning started the fire yesterday evening. The sheriff's department reports three hundred families have been evacuated from their homes in the canyons to the east of Paradise Valley. All roads into the fire area have been closed since midnight. Firefighters hope the fire will be contained by this evening, but for now, the blaze remains out of control.

"The weather is next, after these words from our sponsors."

"Ten thousand acres," Alex murmured. That seemed like a huge area.

"That is it. I am leaving," Irina announced. "If the roads are closed, there will be no rescue. It is time to save one's self."

Alex moved in front of Irina. "You can't leave now. For two reasons. If the fire's out of control, it could go anywhere. There's no way to outrun it. Here we have food and water—and the swimming pool."

"That is not good enough." Irina clenched her jaw. "It is not safe to stay in the fire zone."

"I agree." Alex looked straight into Irina's eyes. "But we have to stay here. By now, our families will have realized that we didn't get evacuated with the others. When they send someone after us, we have to be where they can find us."

"But the roads are closed. No one can get here."

"The police can still get here, if the road is passable." Alex squeezed Irina's arm to reassure her. "They just don't want sightseers interfering with the firefighters. And they *really* don't want to have to rescue someone who shouldn't have been in the fire zone in the first place."

Nicole flashed Irina a big grin. "Maybe they'll

send a helicopter after us. That would be cool. There's plenty of room to land one around here."

"That will never happen." Irina still had a stubborn scowl on her face. Even so, Alex thought they had talked her out of leaving—for now.

"Shhh," Janie said. "The weather is on."

"Your Paradise Valley weather forecast for the next twenty-four hours calls for more of the same. Conditions will remain hot and dry, with gusty winds up to fifty miles an hour. Yesterday's high of one hundred and ten degrees broke the all-time record for the day set in nineteen forty-six. The five-day forecast looks substantially the same, with temperatures above the century mark at least until next weekend."

Laura groaned. "Turn that thing off. I don't want to hear any more bad news."

Alex felt a sinking feeling in her stomach. Hot, dry, and windy was absolutely the worst possible weather right now. To make matters worse, the smoke had settled into the canyon, keeping the visibility down to only a few yards and making it almost impossible for them to call attention to themselves. *How can things get any worse?* she wondered.

*   *   *

"Yes, Mrs. Mack. I understand your concern." Sheriff McGrew ran a hand over his iron gray crew cut. His face was drawn from lack of sleep. "But I don't see anything in these papers that proves the girls weren't evacuated with everybody else from that area. You yourself said the house was checked off on the list. That means everybody was accounted for. Those kids probably walked out of the evac center before anyone wrote down their names. It happens *every time* we do this. Kids are always sneaking off in the confusion, going to the mall or visiting friends without getting permission. I don't have the manpower available to do half what needs doing, let alone chase teenagers who're playing hooky."

Mrs. Mack retrieved the stack of papers she had given the sheriff. "Is this your final word?" she asked. Annie, seated beside her mother, winced at the dangerous tone in her mother's voice, honed by years of working with Danielle Atron. Annie knew not to cross her when Mrs. Mack used that tone.

McGrew closed his eyes briefly. "I've done everything I can for you, Mrs. Mack. You're not the only one who needs help. I've got a call out for the deputy who evacuated Pedregoso Canyon. I'll let you know which center the girls were taken to. Now I've got work to do. Will you *please* let me do it?"

"Very well. I'll be sure your name figures prominently in what I tell the newspapers." Mrs. Mack's voice shook on the last words. She strode quickly from the room.

With shock, Annie saw tears of frustration in her mother's eyes. She closed the door behind them and broke into a jog to catch her mother. "What do we do next? We've been trying all morning to get someone to listen to us."

"I have one more idea," Mrs. Mack said, rubbing her hand across her eyes. Her heels tapped a staccato rhythm down the front stairs of the stationhouse. "One I should have thought of a long time ago."

The others were arguing over the wisdom of making a flag from a bedsheet while Alex and Nicole collected their gear. "It will just catch fire and burn up," Robyn said.

"But we need something big enough to be seen from the air. Our only chance is for a plane flying over us to see our signal," Laura replied.

"Then we have to find something that won't burn!" Robyn insisted.

"Why don't you look for alternatives instead of arguing?" Nicole asked as she and Alex ducked out the door. "If you don't find anything else, *then* you can decide if the sheet idea is too risky."

"Do you think they'll do that?" Alex asked as she steadied the ladder for Nicole.

The other girl shrugged. "What I think is—if we don't get rescued soon, they'll *really* start fighting with each other. Everybody's getting too jumpy to listen to reason."

Alex turned on the water and followed Nicole up the ladder. In the daylight, Alex had no trouble seeing the results of her night's work. The roof was speckled with dozens of black spots, ranging from tiny up to the size of her hand. If she hadn't kept the shingles wet, any of those patches might have turned into a fire that could have destroyed the house.

Nicole touched a large scorched spot. "This shouldn't have burned so quickly. I wonder if these shingles are up to snuff."

"You sound like Robyn. Don't go borrowing trouble."

The girls laughed and started to work. Once suggested, Alex couldn't get Nicole's idea out of her head. Laura had said the roof was replaced by someone willing to cut corners. Could he have used shingles that weren't properly fireproofed?

"Hey, guys!" Tanya shouted. "We found some dry water paint. How big do we need to make the SOS?"

With Alex and Nicole shouting directions, four of the girls marked the corners of each letter while Janie spread the powdered paint between them. When they were done, twenty-foot-high letters in rainbow colors spelled "SOS" on the front lawn.

Alex gave Janie a thumbs-up signal. "It looks great! If the smoke clears for a few minutes, someone is bound to see that."

"I hope," she added in a low voice to Nicole. "We need something to go our way."

"Amen to that." Nicole turned back to soaking the shingles. "It can't be a minute too soon for me."

CHAPTER 10

An hour later the wind shifted direction and began to blow harder. The thick pall of smoke shredded and the tatters began to disperse. Laura and Tanya cheered, but Janie looked worried. "That wind is from the southeast. It could blow the fire back toward us over the area that didn't burn last night."

"Spoilsport!" Tanya slapped palms with Laura. "Before that, someone will see our SOS and get us out of here."

"I'm going up on the roof to take a look around."

Janie joined Alex and Nicole on the roof. "Is it really as bad as you said?" Alex asked as Janie fastened her safety line. "Or were you trying to scare them?"

"We'll know as soon as the smoke clears a little more. That southeast wind is the worst. It blows the hardest and the longest."

Before long, it was clear that Janie wasn't imagining the danger. The leading edge of the fire was racing toward them over dry, unburned grass dotted with scrubby brush. When the wind changed earlier, the fire had moved back into the mountains and burned southward. But with the latest change in direction, the wind was no longer blowing across the burned-out areas.

Nicole swallowed. "We'd better warn the others and get ready for the pool. Can anyone tell how long we have?"

As the flames marched toward them, Alex felt an idea take form. Maybe, just maybe, there was a way she could get help for them. "Janie, where does your water come from?"

"This area has its own system. The original owner put a reservoir up in the mountains. About five years ago, the property owners in the canyon upgraded the pumping station. It's the best in the area now." She gave Alex a lopsided grin. "We shouldn't run out of water, if that's what you mean."

"No. I mean . . ." Alex scrambled to come up with a plausible explanation for her question. She'd been thinking about morphing and trying to reach the pumping station to summon help. But with the canyon on its own system, the chances were small that the phones would be working at the pumping station. "I wondered if you were on the main Paradise Valley system. Someone might notice how much water we're using and come get us."

Janie shook her head. "Nice idea. But we're not."

Alex forced a cheerful smile. "But the good news is, we have plenty of water to hold off the fire."

"Until the firefighters start using it." Nicole shook her head. "My uncle says, when they're fighting a big fire, they grab any water they can get. How long do you think it will be until they drop in a chopper to drain your reservoir?"

"That will take some doing. However, the backup generator at the pumping station could run out of fuel." Janie gave the fire a last look and headed for the ladder. "No pumps, no water. We'd better get everything soaked down now, just in case."

As she watched Janie climb down the ladder,

Alex told herself that morphing and traveling through the water lines was a dumb idea. She'd never stayed in liquid form even half as long as she'd need to get out of Pedregoso Canyon. It would be disastrous if she changed back to human form inside a pipe.

And that wasn't her only problem. The other girls would notice she was missing. They might even search for her, which could have fatal consequences if somebody got caught by the fire. The final obstacle—and the hardest for her— would be to explain how she alone managed to get out of Pedregoso Canyon.

It would have been worth the risk, if she could have sent help. Given Janie's explanation of the water system, success seemed unlikely. Reluctantly, Alex concluded that she would do her friends more good by remaining with them.

Alex turned back to her work. The wind was blowing sparks over the house. The smoke swirled and billowed across the canyon. One moment they could see almost a mile and the next, only a few feet. During the clear periods, Alex spotted the tanker planes dumping chemicals far to the south. Now, when the pilots should see their SOS without the smoke, the planes were too far away.

Alex wondered if she could make the SOS more visible. If she morphed, maybe she could use her body like a mirror to send a signal. She didn't know how long she could do that, though. If someone didn't see her flashes immediately, the others would notice she was missing.

She couldn't risk sending up a zapper, either, even though the pilots could finally see it. The other girls would see it, too, and that would expose her powers.

Wait a minute! Alex shook her head, wondering how stupid she could be. Mr. Robertson had more emergency supplies than she had ever dreamed existed. He should have some flares in his collection. "Robyn!" she yelled. "Were there any flares in that stuff you went through?"

Robyn poked her head out of the garage, her face almost as white as her mask. "I don't remember seeing any, but I didn't get through all the boxes earlier."

Alex pointed toward the planes. "If we can see them, they might be able to see a flare."

"I'll look." Robyn disappeared into the garage.

Alex crossed her fingers. It made sense to shoot off flares when the planes were visible.

Everybody would see them and know what was happening. She hadn't thought about looking for flares earlier, and that was just as well. With the area shrouded in smoke, using flares would have meant wasting a limited resource.

She settled into her routine of spraying any sparks that landed, then jumping to the next danger zone. The flat, smoky brightness of the daylight made it difficult to see the sparks. Sometimes she didn't know a batch had landed until she heard them sizzle on the damp shingles. At other times, she didn't catch them until a wisp of smoke twisted upward from the roof.

At first Alex wasn't sure the water pressure was dropping. It happened so slowly it took a while for her to notice. She tried to move more water with her telekinetic power, but there wasn't enough water in the system to replace what she lifted out.

She looked to see what the others were doing. Janie and Laura had one hose stretched into the trees south of the house. They were soaking down a buffer between the walnut grove and the approaching fire, but they were having the same problem as Alex. Only a trickle of water came from the hose.

Nicole and Irina were shoveling dirt on the

fires started by sparks that landed in the dry grass. Tanya was dragging a third hose back to the house. Her slumped shoulders told Alex that she had given up trying to get enough water to do any good.

"Turn it off!" Janie yelled to Robyn. "This isn't working."

Alex realized they were giving her all the water for the roof. Even so, it wasn't enough. She had the only hose in use, and she was getting less than a quarter of the water that had been flowing earlier. If the pressure continued to drop, it wouldn't be long before she couldn't get any water, even with her powers.

The wind pushed a cloud of smoke over the house. It was so thick Alex couldn't see the ground. She took a step, stumbled, and fell to her knees. Without her cleats to hold her, she started sliding. She dropped the hose and grabbed for something to slow her fall. Her hands slipped off the damp shingles.

Her safety line jerked Alex to a stop, forcing the air from her lungs. She tried to catch her breath and started coughing. The smoke burned her eyes and made her lungs ache. She didn't know how much more of this she could take.

Slowly, Alex inched her way up her safety line

to the ridge of the roof. Carefully, she eased herself to her feet and looked around. *Is it worth retrieving the hose?* she wondered.

A gust of wind stirred the smoke. For an instant, Alex could see more than a few feet. The flames were creeping toward the grove, just yards from where Tanya and Irina had been working a few minutes ago. Their firebreak wasn't going to hold.

"Run for the pool!" Janie shouted. She and Laura raced through the trees toward the house.

Alex looked for the others, but she couldn't see them. Would they see if she morphed and flowed through the gutters to the pool? It seemed likely that someone would catch her.

That meant she had to take the hard way down. Alex unclipped her safety line. She was still shaky from her near accident. In spite of that, she forced her rubbery legs to carry her to the ladder.

Climbing down was easier. With each rung, she reminded herself she was that much closer to safety. When she reached the ground, though, she had a decision to make. The shortest way to the pool was around the end of the house nearest the fire.

Racing at top speed, she turned the other way.

She didn't know if anything was burning in that direction, but it seemed her best chance.

As she rounded the corner, she saw several blazing trees. Waves of heat rolled toward her. The smoke burned her throat and made it difficult for her to breathe. The flames roared and crackled, mocking her efforts to outrun them.

It was too late to go back the other way. The fire had almost certainly blocked that way, too. Summoning her last bit of energy, Alex poured on the speed.

A loud crack erupted from the heart of the inferno. In slow motion, the largest tree toppled straight for Alex. Desperately, she shoved it with her powers. It continued to fall, missing Alex but crashing directly in front of her. The trunk shattered and a cloud of sparks burst into the air.

Alex skidded to a halt. She was trapped. There was no way she could get around the fallen tree.

CHAPTER 11

Alex stared at the fallen tree in horror. It lay across her only route to safety. She heard screams and splashes as the other girls jumped into the pool and swam away from the fire. The smoke burned her eyes and blurred her vision. Angrily, she dashed away the tears. *How am I going to get out of this?*

A closer look showed gaps between the pieces of the trunk. Most of them were small, but one looked big enough to slip through—if she morphed.

She moved closer, studying the spot. The two chunks of wood were lying at angles to each other. The larger piece was propped up on the ends of two branches. In liquid form, she could fit through the gap. It was her best shot at escaping from the fire. If she hurried, she could slide into the pool and re-form against the colored tile before anybody missed her.

Her decision made, Alex morphed into a puddle and raced through the gap. Bits of flaming debris dropped in her way, forcing her to dodge back and forth to avoid being hit. She didn't know what damage the burning twigs might cause to her liquid body, and she didn't want to find out.

The surface beneath her changed from the lumpy gravel walkway to the smoother bricks around the pool. Gathering her energy, she raced for the water at top speed. She oozed over the edge and poured into the water. With relief, she saw the other girls were at the far end of the pool, looking toward the house and yelling her name.

The growl of a plane's engines rolled toward her. A tanker plane, moving low and slow, appeared above the house. It dumped chemicals on the house and the burning trees. The flames sputtered and burned lower. Even through the distortions of seeing in her liquid form, Alex rec-

ognized the logo of the Paradise Valley Chemical plant.

They make useful *chemicals,* she thought in
amazement. She had become so involved in her
personal game of hide-and-seek with the chemical plant that she had forgotten they made other
things than GC-161.

She thought the pilot had probably seen her
friends. However, she didn't want to take any
chances. She was sure she could tilt her liquid
body to send flashes of light toward the pilot.
She shifted her body back and forth, hoping she
was catching enough light to be seen.

The plane wagged its wings. Relief surged
through Alex. She knew what that meant from
a gliding lesson she had taken last year. She had
finally caught somebody's attention. The pilot
knew where they were.

Cheers erupted from the far end of the pool.
Quickly, while the others were distracted, Alex
slid beneath the water and re-formed. She
popped to the surface, gasping for breath.

"Hey, Alex!" Nicole shouted. "Did you see the
plane? We're going to be rescued."

"I saw, Nicole." Alex pulled herself along the
side of the pool until she reached the others. Her
near escape left her feeling too shaky to swim.

Should she make up an alibi for her signal? she wondered. "Since I was down there by myself, I tried to splash out an SOS. But I don't think the pilot saw me."

"Probably not." Nicole rolled over and floated on her back. "Besides, he was flying so low he could hardly miss us."

"And all those chemicals should keep the fire from burning the house," Janie said. "They may even save most of the trees."

Irina was floating low in the water, with only her face exposed. "I do not intend to test that theory. I am staying in the water until someone arrives to rescue us."

To Alex, that sounded like a fine idea. She'd had her fill of firefighting. The water was cool and soothing after her hard work. She decided not to move until their rescuers showed up.

Fifteen minutes later a small, sleek helicopter appeared out of the smoky air and circled over the house. "That's"—Nicole squinted in disbelief—"that's Danielle Atron's executive helicopter."

The helicopter circled lower and disappeared on the other side of the house. The sound of the rotors lowered in pitch.

"I think he landed." Janie pulled herself out

of the pool. "There might be enough room on the lawn."

"For that size, definitely." Nicole followed Janie, beckoning to the others. "Come on. I think that's our ride."

When the girls came around the house, the helicopter was sitting on the lawn. Its rotors were spinning at a very slow rate. The pilot held up four fingers, beckoning to the girls.

"He can only take four of us," Nicole translated. "Whoever wants to go, keep low like they do on *M*A*S*H*."

Janie and Alex exchanged looks. Now that she knew how she was getting out, it didn't seem so important to be the first one. "We'll wait for the next trip," Alex said.

"Everyone else, follow me." Nicole crouched and ran for the helicopter, keeping as close to the ground as she could. While the other girls scrambled for seats, she talked to the pilot.

Nicole ran back to Janie and Alex. The helicopter's rotors spun up, and the sound became deafening. Nicole motioned for them to get down until the helicopter was airborne.

"The pilot says he'll be back in about half an hour. We probably should get back in the pool, just in case."

"Where did you learn about helicopters?" Alex asked as they slid into the water.

"I got to fly a couple of times with my uncle. The first thing you learn, before you get near the chopper, is the safety rules." She looked at Alex and shook her head. "You wouldn't *believe* how dangerous those little things are."

Alex shuddered. She had been so relieved about being rescued that she hadn't considered the risks of flying in a helicopter.

Nicole laughed at Alex's reaction. "We're lucky. Now that the pilot has seen the place and knows we'll follow the rules, there are lots of smaller spaces he can land in. If he has to, he can practically balance it on the edge of the swimming pool while we get in."

Despite Nicole's dire predictions, the three girls stayed put in the swimming pool until the helicopter circled over them and again landed on the lawn. Alex was delighted that she ended up in the front seat, with a view out the front bubblelike canopy. The interior of the chopper was functional and much simpler than Alex had expected.

"Everybody strap down and put your safety

helmets on," the pilot shouted. He was a middle-aged man with "Jim" on his flight suit.

Alex slipped her helmet on, then sorted out her harness straps. The previous occupant had left them in a twisted mess.

"Of course, you all realize that regulations require you to be wearing fireproof flight suits," Jim's voice said through the speakers in Alex's helmet. He gave a soft chuckle. "Under the circumstances, I think we can safely assume that you're willing to waive that requirement."

"Yes!" the three girls said in unison.

"Then we're off."

The rotors speeded up and the sound rose in pitch. They scooted upward on a long diagonal, following the driveway while the helicopter gained altitude and airspeed.

As they cleared the trees, Alex got a good look at the fire zone. Most of it was hidden by smoke. Where the wind had torn holes in the thick haze, the hills were blackened and charred. Miraculously, although the fire had reached the edge of Pedregoso Canyon in several places, it had been stopped at the edge.

Jim waved toward the canyon. "We used this area as a field test for some new firefighting chemicals being developed at the plant. The results were even better than the company hoped." Alex could hear the pride in his voice.

Tanker planes and helicopters were flying to and from the fire zone. Alex shook her head in amazement. She knew how hard she and her friends had worked to keep the fire away from the Robertsons' house. That effort was being repeated on a tremendous scale along the mountain front—all for a fire caused by a single bolt of lightning.

The helicopter settled down onto the landing pad at the chemical plant. A nurse hustled the girls inside and insisted on giving them a checkup. Alex fought her panic. She did *not* want to be examined by anyone on the plant's payroll.

To her relief, the nurse gave her a once-over for burns and blisters. After warning Alex about the dangers and symptoms of smoke inhalation, she released her.

Her parents were waiting outside. "Alex!" While Mr. Mack told Janie and Nicole that their families were waiting at the Mack house, Alex's mother pulled her into a big hug. "Alex, we're so glad you're safe!"

"I'm sure glad to see you!" Alex's face went

hot. She ducked her head until the glow faded. Luckily, nobody noticed.

"You wouldn't believe the trouble we had," Mr. Mack said. "It took hours to convince anyone that you girls had been missed."

Mrs. Mack shook her head. "It is amazingly hard to convince someone with a list that his list is wrong."

"We probably would still be trying, if your mother hadn't asked Ms. Atron to send her executive helicopter after you." Mr. Mack beamed with pride at his wife's ingenuity.

"I was tired of arguing with people who weren't listening to what I said." Mrs. Mack threw her arm around Alex's shoulders and drew her toward the car. Janie and Nicole were already in the backseat. "The others have already gone home. You girls look like you could use a shower and something to eat."

"That sounds like a good idea. . . . And thanks, Mom, for getting us rescued."

Mrs. Mack gave Alex an embarrassed grin. "From what the other girls said, you were doing a good job of keeping the situation under control. We would have worried a lot more if Annie hadn't told us you were planning to use the pool to hide from the fire."

"I'm still glad you got us out when you did." Alex slid into the car beside Nicole. "We were starting to get a little nervous about the fire."

"Yes, thanks for the help, Mr. and Mrs. Mack," Nicole said. "When it comes to brush fires, I prefer to listen to my uncle's stories. This was more firsthand experience than I wanted."

Janie shook her head. Her mouth twisted into a rueful grin. "I just wanted to have a party to celebrate getting my lifeguard certificate. This wasn't at all what I had in mind."

"Well, Janie, I know one thing for sure." Alex grinned at her. "This is one slumber party that I will *never* forget."

About the Author

V. E. (VICKI) MITCHELL has written a *Starfleet Academy* book, *Atlantis Station*, for young readers, two adult *Star Trek* novels—*Enemy Unseen* and *Windows on a Lost World*—and one *Star Trek: The Next Generation* novel, *Imbalance*. In addition to her other Nickelodeon title, *Are You Afraid of the Dark: The Tale of the Bad-Tempered Ghost*, she has also had short stories and articles about writing published in a variety of places. When she isn't writing fiction, she works as a geologist for the Idaho Geological Survey, where her geological publications far exceed her fiction credits. Her hobbies include making costumes, dancing, photography, Chinese cooking, putting on science fiction conventions, and working on her Ph.D. She is married and is working to civilize her new pound puppy, Shilo.

Sometimes, it takes a kid to solve a good crime....

Original stories based on the hit Nickelodeon show!

#1 A Slash in the Night
by Alan Goodman

#2 Takeout Stakeout
By Diana G. Gallagher

#3 Hot Rock
by John Peel

#4 Rock 'n' Roll Robbery
by Lydia C. Marano and David Cody Weiss

#5 Cut and Run
by Diana G. Gallagher

To find out more about *The Mystery Files of Shelby Woo* or any other Nickelodeon show, visit Nickelodeon Online on America Online (Keyword: NICK) and on the Web at www.nick.com.

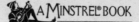

A MINSTREL® BOOK

Published by Pocket Books

1338-05

NICKELODEON/MINSTREL BOOKS POINTS PROGRAM

Official Rules

1. **HOW TO COLLECT POINTS**: Points may be collected by purchasing books in the following series, *The Secret World of Alex Mack*™, *Are You Afraid of the Dark?*, and *The Mystery Files of Shelby Woo*™. Only books in the series published March 1998 and after are eligible for program. Points can be redeemed for merchandise by completing the coupons (found in the back of the books) and mailing with a check or money order in the exact amount to cover postage and handling to Nickelodeon/Minstrel Points Program, P.O. Box 7777-G140, Mt. Prospect, IL 60056-7777. Each coupon is worth 5 points. Copies of coupons are not valid. Simon & Schuster is not responsible for lost, late, illegible, incomplete, stolen, postage-due, or misdirected mail.

2. **40 POINT MINIMUM**: Each redemption request must contain a minimum of 40 points, or 8 coupons, in order to redeem for merchandise. Limit one merchandise request per envelope: 8 coupons (40 points), 12 coupons (60 points), 15 coupons (75 points), or 20 coupons (100 points).

3. **ELIGIBILITY**: Open to legal residents of the United States (excluding Puerto Rico) and Canada (excluding Quebec) only. Void where taxed, licensed, restricted, or prohibited by law. Redemption requests from groups, clubs, or organizations will not be honored.

4. **DELIVERY**: Allow 6-8 weeks for delivery of merchandise.

5. **MERCHANDISE**: All merchandise is subject to availability and may be replaced with an item of merchandise of equal or greater value at the sole discretion of Simon & Schuster.

6. **ORDER DEADLINE**: All redemption requests must be received by January 31, 1999, or while supplies last. Offer may not be combined with any other promotional offer from Simon & Schuster. Employees and the immediate family members of such employees of Simon & Schuster, its parent company, subsidiaries, divisions and related companies and their respective agencies and agents are ineligible to participate.

COMPLETE THE COUPON AND MAIL TO
NICKELODEON/MINSTREL POINTS PROGRAM
P.O. BOX 7777-G140
MT. PROSPECT, IL 60056-7777

NAME_____

ADDRESS_____

CITY _____ STATE _____ ZIP _____

THIS COUPON WORTH FIVE POINTS
Offer expires January 31, 1999

I have enclosed __ coupons and a check/money order (in U.S. currency only) made payable to "Nickelodeon/Minstrel Books Points Program" to cover postage and handling.

❑ 8 coupons (+ $3.50 postage and handling)   ❑ 15 coupons (+ $3.50 postage and handling)

❑ 12 coupons (+ $3.50 postage and handling)   ❑ 20 coupons (+ $5.50 postage and handling)

1464(2of2)